BEN ROSE

Bury Me Upside Down

This book was professionally typeset on Reedsy.
Find out more at reedsy.com

Dedication
For Get Lost Jimmy who was taken from us too soon, for Top Cat,
and for all the cats and kittens who rocked out at The Core in
Harrisburg, PA
~Ben Rose

Contents

Quote

"When my time on earth is finished, and my mortal deeds are passed, I want they should bury me upside down, so the critics can kiss my ass!"
Anonymous

CHAPTER ONE

17 July, 1993

I sailed the magazine I was reading across the room toward my cherry wood desk. I missed the desktop and it landed on my office chair. If you must know, the magazine was the Christmas issue of *SNACK TRAYS* from my private stash. My parents don't have a clue that I own a stash of girlie magazines. Then again, it often amazes me how little they do know. They act like they were never kids once. Maybe they weren't.

Easing myself off the bed, I ambled over to the window and opened my black and grey checkered curtains. Staring out the bay window at the lush green trees, and perfectly manicured lawn, I sighed a deep mooing sound reminiscent of a bull in heat. A bull in heat was an apt description of my mental and physical state.

I turned my ceiling fan to high, grabbed my black sketch book, and doodled a few images; poplar leaves, chrysanthemums, and vines intertwined with each other on a large gate with a sign reading "Abandon all hope, ye who enter this domain." With extreme care, I colored in the leaves with pastels. I emphasized the dark but left a few unshaded highlights to present a natural feel.

Probably, I thought to myself with a growing sense of angst,

I'd be better off if someone sprinkled cow shit on me. Plants seem to thrive on it.

When I was seven, I purchased a fetid, little fern plant at a street fair for Mother's Day. It was all I could afford at the time. The plant was dying and needed someone to love and tend to it. It looked neglected like an urchin who has never been to the park, or zoo, or anywhere nice. I gave the fern to my mother, and she took over from there.

With her assortment of plant remedies, and do-hickeys used for gardening, she made the pathetic thing grow. That fern grew into a beautiful plant. She talked to it in her sweetest voice and told it what a good plant it was. She loved that plant like it was the child she always wanted.

I imagine she talked to me that way once upon a time, but those days ended with elementary school. Once I completed sixth grade, my folks sent me to the Valley of Hinnom Institute. Sounds like a prison, no? It wasn't – not exactly. VHI was an academic academy for youth grades seven through twelve. I fit in that range somewhere, depending on the class. I tested higher in English and art, lower in math and science.

My parents thought the place exceptional because the brochure had some crap about, *we encourage free thinking, self-motivation. For a mere $4800.00 a year, we guarantee that upon graduation your little angel will be admitted to some of the finest institutes of higher learning.*

Yeah, right. Believe that, and I would sell you some beach front property in Nebraska. I'd only ask $5000.00 down.

My folks ate up that white-bread claptrap with a spoon. The only free thinking and self-motivation they cared about was me taking care of myself so that they didn't have to be involved in my life. The prestigious university part was also on their

3

radar; not because they cared where I went as much as they cared that their yuppie, WASP friends knew that I was going somewhere prestigious. It was all about reputation with them. I use terms like white-bread and WASP because no better terms will suffice. We happen to be Caucasian and upper-middle class. It isn't my fault I was born into a savage race of oppressors. I was cursed in that way. Starting in seventh grade, I read works by Howard Zinn, Martin Luther King Jr., George Jackson, James Welch, Amiri Baraka, and others of that caliber. I knew the truth about my race and the abhorrent things we did to other races.

I'll admit that VHI had some merits. There was a better than average English department, and I had an outstanding art teacher. The rest of the student body I could take or leave. Not that some of the student bodies didn't deserve a second look. There were some nicely packed rumps, shapely legs, and well-constructed breasts, not to mention beautiful faces. As for intelligence, until this past summer I wasn't as concerned with the feminine mind.

My favorite teacher was a guy the students called Mr. K. I wasn't sure what the K stood for. It might have been just a K. He was the Artistic Creativity Coordinator. Like a janitor is a Custodial Engineer. Mr. K. encouraged me to draw, write poetry, and escape reality through various activities. Nothing illegal or nefarious, mind you. During class we played Dungeons and Dragons or pretended to be various objects around the room. Engagement of that sort.

"The best way to know your subject is to be your subject." Mr. K. always said.

A month into the past school year I found this book at the library by Dr. Timothy Leary that was based on the Tibetan Book

4

of The Dead. I read it, I also read a book by Terrence McKenna. After studying these two authors, I asked Mr. K. if I should try psychonautic means to expand my creative scope.

"That's entirely up to you, my friend. If so, do be cautious." He replied.

That wasn't much of an answer, but it's a fair example of how most of the teachers interacted with students. They answered questions with questions and weren't quick to give their own opinions.

Pardon the digression into academic hell. Muttering cute phrases to a boy in his teens is no way to foster independence, ergo my mother didn't do that. She only talked to her plants that way. When I got to feeling like emotional refuse, she'd glare at me and say "Grow up and deal with your own problems. Quit whining about life you ungrateful, little brat. I won't be here forever, you know. Got to die sometime. You can't forever be running to your mommy to solve your problems. Learn to suck it up and solve your own problems."

This was typical of how my parental units dealt with me. They operated under the belief that by pushing me away they were making me more self-reliant. Instead, I stopped trusting them. I stopped turning to them for much of anything. That was where the trouble really began.

Many times, I wished I were an eagle; a majestic bird soaring over the landscape, surveying the earth from on high. If I were an eagle then I wouldn't be stuck in my bedroom like a prisoner, ruminating about what happened this past summer, so scared I could puke. I'd be free. There would be nothing behind me and everything ahead of me.

The past summer was the best one I had ever known. It was also the worst one I had ever known. I made some new friends; people who truly needed me. They were dying inside, and I revived them. I gave them renewed life in much the same way my mother tended to her plants. I met some people who demonstrated the flaws in my supposition that all adults are the enemy. However, I also I met some adults who completely reaffirmed that belief.

My new friends and I planned a coup, and made it happen. Just last week, a killer night I will never forget if I live to see thirty. I may never see any of those friends again, but I changed the world — my corner of it, in any case — for an hour at least. The moon was full, the music was pulsating, and the plants were blooming so bright a body could feel it at a soul deep level. My friends and I took a stand, and made our voices heard.

Andy Warhol may have been correct that people only get fifteen minutes of fame. Mine came that night. Like as not I shall never see another night as powerful. Now I am doing hard time in my bedroom as an exchange for those fifteen minutes. Freedom costs, and those willing to stand up must pay the price where the cost is dear.

The rest of that glorious night was a mess. Police cars converged with their flashers and spinners, newspaper reporters were shouting questions at everyone, and a well-constructed beauty with a good-sized rack showed up to broadcast everything live on the late news. I was handcuffed with Dawn, placed into the back of a car, taken to the local precinct, and booked for disturbing the peace and inciting a riot amongst other charges.

My parents were called to come collect me. They had been pulled out of bed. Few people, outside of family and friends, had ever seen my parents show much emotion. They'd put on an act for outsiders of being even-keel and logical in all their affairs. That night, however, they outdid themselves emotionally.

When my parents arrived at the station, they made a big production of being June and Ward Cleaver. They told the police that they couldn't imagine how their upstanding son could be involved in anything like a riot. My mother even hugged me to demonstrate her concern.

Once we got home, that act changed. With no one around to observe them, they became once more the parents to whom I was accustomed. In short, all Hell broke loose.

As I've indicated, my parents definitely weren't Ozzie and Harriet. They were absorbed in their own lives and didn't want to be involved in mine beyond the basic requirement of providing shelter, clothing, and food.

My parents rarely lost their tempers, but once they did it was game over. That night was one of the occasions where they completely lost their cool. My mother told me what an ungrateful bastard I was; how much I damaged their reputation in the community, while my father slapped me and shoved me around the room.

This was also the summer where I was deflowered, assuming that a guy can be. That word is more often associated with a girl surrendering her maiden status to a boy for the first time. Mr. K. once informed me that all people are both male and female. It's a yin and yang equation, as well as a biological fact upon conception. At some point we do become one thing or another; at least physically. So, perhaps, deflowered is the right word.

My mental circuits were jumpy, I was growing angrier with each passing hour, and I couldn't focus my thoughts being cooped up in my room with the desk, chair, bed covered in a black and grey comforter, and walk in closet. I heard people coming and going downstairs. All week long there were conferences in the living room. My father was a lawyer and served as my legal attorney. That wasn't my choice, but no one asked for my input.

From my window I could see people arrive and leave. Police officers, lawyers, child psychologists. One of the latter was Cassandra Larkspur, a know-it-all, self-proclaimed child expert with inane ideas about getting in touch with your feelings. Her radio show had a wide local following, but I knew what she was the first time I listened in.

Dr. Larkspur may have sounded authoritative when she spoke of getting in touch with one's feelings, but I was certain that the bitch hadn't had a feeling in over fifty years. Probably hadn't had a good feel in fifteen of those years, either. I know for a fact that her daughter, Dawn, hated her with a passion. That daughter was trapped in her own room ten blocks to the west.

I didn't even want to think about Dawn. I had enough internal pressure, and if I thought about her too much, I knew I would blow. I was in love; deeply, passionately, bases loaded bottom of the ninth inning in the world series, head over heels in love. It wasn't supposed to be that way, but I'll get to that.

The adults came and went downstairs, discussing what would happen to me. That's why I wrote this account of what happened. I had to make clear the facts that belie the rumors and gossip the press was printing. I wanted to set the record straight before I was silenced for most of the rest of my life. The following is the truth whether it happened like I say it did or not.

CHAPTER TWO

To set the record straight from the start, I began using my nom-de-guerre long before the trouble commenced. It wasn't an alias like the reporters claimed. It was like this; I was born Francis Leslie Ahriman. That name might have been OK for a boy when Shakespeare was around, or even President Eisenhower, but not in the present day.

First, the name is stuffy and pretentious. One tends to get tormented over a name like that, and then it comes to blows. Speaking of blows, the name is effeminate. It belongs to someone who minces around and speaks with an affected lisp. I got tired of having teachers call me out by my full name in class, and then having to punch some cool-guy idiot in the mouth later in the bathrooms or on the playground.

So, I changed my name. I started calling myself Cyrus Ahriman. Cyrus was a Persian king, and founder of the Achaemenid Empire. There was also Cyrus who ran the biggest gang in New York City, according to Sol Yurick. Cyrus was, therefore, a powerful name, and I felt that it fit me better. The name change wasn't legal, but it also wasn't a criminal alias.

There was no way that I could have legally changed my name. When my father spoke to me at all, he berated me, or he issued orders. He was the consummate alpha male. I don't recall having many meaningful discussions even when I was a child. We sure as hell weren't going to discuss my not liking my name. His grandfather was named Francis and my mother's grandfather was Leslie. Of course, that was back in the day when the white race was oppressing everyone who wasn't white; enslaving them or forcing them onto reservations. I suppose that it didn't matter in those days if your name could be mistaken for female.

I joined a local gym and signed up as Cyrus Ahriman. I was stopped on the street and asked to sign a petition indicating that the president should be allowed to serve three terms instead of two. I couldn't even vote for three years, but I signed Cyrus Ahriman on the proper line. When I signed up for art classes at the local museum, I signed the form, Cyrus Ahriman.

Incidentally, the class was taught by Mr. K. from my high school. He said that he liked my new name, that I was finding myself. I didn't have a clue what that meant, but it sounded good. It also sounded good that my participation in the class counted as credit toward early graduation.

I decided that my new life would be full of action, adventure, ethos, pathos, and cosmos. To an outsider that might have sounded incredible, but it fit with the town in which I resided. As far as I knew, everyone was a yuppie or high-priced executive. I'd never seen much else, except in the park.

My father, as I said, was a lawyer. My mother was a botanist. She also had the periodic table memorized forward and backward and calculated math equations in her head better than an adding machine. One would have thought her the most put-together and perceptive person. She wasn't. She had an assistant who kept track of her appointments. She had another assistant who catalogued her research. She had Mrs. Ferrigno to keep track of her household, and her son.

Mrs. Louise Ferrigno was hired fifteen years ago when I was born. She cooked, cleaned, kept track of the household budget, and was supposed to keep watch over me. She was such a space cadet that I wound up keeping track of her. She was short and dumpy, with a wrinkled visage, and calloused hands. She was a sweet old lady but had the attention span of a hummingbird. My parents never noticed, somehow.

Mrs. Ferrigno watched talk shows most of the day. You know the type, *Russian Mail Order Brides* today on Donahue, or *Love Fest Flops* next on Jerry Springer. Mrs. Ferrigno would often invite me to watch with her, and she'd spend the entire show commenting on the perverts who appeared.

To her a pervert was anyone who was gay, divorced, living with a partner outside of wedlock, who belonged to an Eastern religion, or who in anyway didn't fit into her own secluded world. She was always good to me, but she could also be narrow-minded. I found that most white people were, whether they admitted it or not. I had a working hypothesis that the problem was genetic. Caucasian people were born narrow-minded and lacking in decency.

When not watching TV, Mrs. Ferrigno read romance novels. These were nothing more than salacious and raunchy soap operas set to the written page. The books, which resembled a literary form of the magazines I collected, were a natural extension of her talk-show pastime. The main characters were always named Veronica, or Josephine, or some such moniker. They were large busted, tightly packaged wenches who wound up with evil men called Lord Greggory or Prince Stephan.

Mrs. Ferrigno read to me from the books on occasion, and I

11

swore that if the books had been just a tad filthier, they would have been published by Larry Flynt. The content was loose on plot and character development, and big on sexual scenes. Not that I objected to sexual anything, but why read about it when you're too old to be involved.

When not engaged in this sex-fest or her shows, Mrs. Ferrigno actually did clean our house. She was good at it; better than I could hope to be. The problem was that she was forgetful. I mean, she would sometimes forget where she was. She'd be standing in place with the vacuum running, staring into space. I'd have to remind her to move the machine.

Her reading wasn't limited to romance novels, either. On rainy days we'd sit and eat Cajun corn chips, drink grape soda, and chat about literature. In her youth, Mrs. Ferrigno had read extensively. She was familiar with classics like *Their Eyes Were Watching God*, *Go Tell It on the Mountain*, *Naked Lunch*, and *On the Road*.

One Day we were discussing Shakespeare's *Twelfth Night*, when she said, "I forget to tell you that you received a telephone call this morning. Someone wants you to babysit."

"OK." I nodded. "Who was it, and when do they want me to show up?"

That was when Mrs. Ferrigno went glassy eyed, and her forehead scrunched. It was a sure sign that she had forgotten something. My parents never noticed, but Mrs. Ferrigno had a brain like a colander. Her brain slowly drained of all its contents. She got this odd look, like she was stoned or something. She'd wring her hands, and her brow would furrow. I became an expert on handling the situation.

"Calm down. Take a deep breath." I spoke in a soft monotone. "Think back. Phone rang. You answered it. They asked for me.

What did they say?"

The look fizzled out a bit. "She said she knew your parents from the club."

"Which club?"

"Oh no!" Glassy eyes, and furrowed brow.

"It doesn't matter. What was her name?" I kept my voice soft and even.

"I wrote it by the phone?"

"Which phone? We have four of them."

"Oh, my stars!" She looked better. "I was washing the dishes and watching Geraldo on the portable set. I wrote the information on the pad by the kitchen phone."

I ran to the kitchen and noticed a box of Cream of Wheat on the washing machine. I ignored it for a moment and grabbed the pad by the phone. It read "Ms. Cramer. Babysit." Next to that was a telephone number.

"Hey, Mrs. F," I said before I called the number, "Why is there a box of Cream of Wheat on the washing machine?"

"Oh, my stars!"

I let go a hearty laugh, "You didn't."

I checked the machine, and all the clothes were covered with Cream of Wheat powder. I removed them and shook each item out over the sink. I replaced the clothes and found the detergent unopened on the side of the stove. I got the laundry started and put things back where they belonged.

"Don't worry, Mrs. F, I took care of it." I called out.

After starting the wash, I made my call to Ms. Cramer. From her voice I imagined all sorts of things about her. Young. Tall. Good looking because she made sure of it before leaving the house. Face lifted, butt reduced, bust enlarged. She was likely a graduate of the finest preparatory schools. Her voice was nasal, and she pronounced each word exactly – hitting the proper emphasis on the right syllable. She wore minimal makeup, ate yoghurt and granola regularly, jogged, rode a bicycle, and marched in rallies – but only so that she could be seen doing so.

Her bicycle would be top of the line, even if she had to forgo other necessities to buy it. Her yoghurt would be Greek because regular yoghurt just would not do. Her outfits would be custom tailored, and she'd make sure everyone knew that they were. It's funny how much a voice on the phone can tell the listener.

I could picture the kid, too. Perfectly groomed, stylish haircut, rosy cheeked, matching sweater and pants, biblical name, and most likely raised on a diet of health food and spring water.

"I heard about your father from some friends of mine, Francis. They were impressed with him and said that he was the right sort. I am certain you know what I mean."

Unfortunately, I knew exactly what she meant. "Yes, ma'am. You need a babysitter, I was told. I'm available. How many children, and what are the hours?"

"I have only one child. A son. The world is populated enough as it is. I have a meeting with clients this afternoon, and I desire to not have Jeremiah under foot. If you could please pick him up, and perhaps take him for a walk in the park, I would be most appreciative."

I knew it would be a biblical name. Take him for a walk in the park? *He's your son, not your toy poodle!* I thought to myself. "Yes, ma'am. That would be fine." I replied.

"Very well. Be here at one-thirty promptly."

"Yes, ma'am. Goodbye."

I had planned to head to the park that afternoon in any case. I thought it was the perfect place to sketch, and to start my new life with my new name. The idea of having a child with me made the plan even better. I enjoyed babysitting. Something inside of me stirred at the notion of being needed and depended upon. Nobody needs a person so much as a small child with wet pants, or a banged-up knee, sniffling and teary eyed, hands in the air begging to be held.

I walked out of the kitchen. "Hey, Mrs. F. I can watch TV with you while we have lunch, but then I have to cut out. I have a job watching a kid this afternoon. I'll leave a note for my parents."

We had tuna salad on lettuce, and iced tea. The guests that day were models who had appeared in adult magazines before changing careers. I recognized two of them from my collection. They were dressed, and unfettered, but the show was interesting anyway.

Three young ladies were brought out who were interested in the business, and the former models tried talking them out of it. One of the aspiring models said that she would go out with any man anytime and do anything he liked. To prove it she left with a man from the front row who was dressed in a suit and tie. I felt a certain concern over her behavior, but I was also jealous. I had never been with a girl, especially not one who would do anything I wanted.

CHAPTER THREE

Jeremiah Carlson Cramer was five years old, with a perfect part in his hair, and wearing Osh-Kosh overalls over a long sleeved, pale pink t-shirt. He looked me over with a great deal of distrust. Ms. Cramer also gave me the once over twice. I had changed into clean jeans, and a polo shirt, but I still felt like a bug under a magnifying glass.

I didn't much care what Ms. Cramer thought, as long as she paid me. I was pleased that Jeremiah was wary. His mother might be a charm school beauty queen with her nose in the air, but this clean and pressed five-year-old boy was none too happy. He was going to be on his guard shaking hands with a boy named Francis.

"Ms. Cramer," I said, giving Jeremiah a chance to size me up, "I prefer to go by my middle name, Cyrus. If you call me at home please ask for Francis, as my parents still call me that. I do hope you understand."

"I do. My parents still refer to me as Lynette when I much prefer Lynn. Jeremiah, this is Cyrus. He will be taking you to the park this afternoon. You will obey him and behave yourself."

"Yes, Mommy. Pleased to meet you, Cyrus." Jeremiah shook my hand. "I'll go put on my sweater." He walked toward the stairs.

A sweater? It's eighty-two degrees outside! I thought to myself.

While we waited, Ms. Cramer began issuing instructions. "No petting animals. You never know if there might be germs."

"Check." I replied.

"Make sure he keeps his sweater on. I do not want him catching cold. He is prone to ear infections."

"Check. Sweater stays on."

"No candy, or other sweets. I have to pay the dental bills if his teeth are full of holes. If he eats between meals, then his appetite is ruined for what I prepare."

"Check. No snacks." I replied. *Wouldn't want to ruin his appetite for rice cakes and bee spit with a side of watercress.* I thought to myself.

Explain to him about not picking flowers in the park. It is against the rules. I certainly want him to appreciate nature, however."

"Got it. No picking flowers."

"No climbing trees. He might fall. The medical bills for that would come out of my pocket. Also, no playing in the public fountain. One never knows what germs the other children may have."

"Understood. No trees. No fountain."

"Most important, he is never to talk to strangers. Lord knows what sort of perverts are in the park. They might kidnap him and do Lord knows what. I saw a group of foreigners the other day. The women looked like umbrella stands with their black facial coverings. The men all had these towels wrapped around their heads. There were also these boys and girls who had earrings in their eyebrows and lips. The girls had their heads shaved."

"Understood."

I waited to see if there were more rules. I found it hard to hide my annoyance. The park was full of interesting people, none of whom would harm a child. They wouldn't accost anyone unless first attacked. She gave me a look that indicated her trust in me as an adult. I appreciated that, but I felt sickened by the clear implications of her words. This was her precious WASP child, and she didn't want him mingling with anyone of a darker race. She didn't want him associating with anyone who didn't fit into her idea of proper society.

Jeremiah returned, skipping down the hallway. His sweater was an exact match for the one Mr. Rogers wore. Ms. Cramer buttoned him into it and kissed him goodbye. She reminded me of the rules and opened the door for us.

Jeremiah and I walked two blocks before stopping. There was a very polite golden retriever laying in a yard, and Jeremiah stopped to pet it. He also petted three cats in the neighboring yard. I saw not reason why he shouldn't. People on my side of town didn't often own attack dogs. Rule one was out the window.

The weather outside was summery. I unbuttoned the kid's sweater and put it in my backpack. Rule two was history.

"Mommy says I have to wear my sweater." Jeremiah informed me.

"Jeremiah," I replied, "You're starting to blanch."

"What's blanch mean?"

"You're getting pale from overheating," I explained. "It's almost eighty-five degrees out for crying out loud! Nobody wears a sweater this time of year."

Three blocks more and we stopped in a corner store. I purchased us each a chocolate bar and a soda. Rule three was down the drain. I didn't see how eating a small snack would ruin the appetite of a growing boy.

Three rules broken before we got to the park. There was another matter as well, but it wasn't technically a rule. Nothing had been said about changing his name. It was Jeremiah's idea and assured me that he and I would get along fine.

"Jeremiah, do you like playing on the swings?" I asked. "I know I sure do."

"Stop calling me that!" He snapped at me. "Please," he added politely.

"Do you prefer Jerry?"

"No! I'm not a mouse. Call me Jack Flash."

I smiled. He watched morning cartoons. Most likely before his mother woke up. *Jack Flash and His Galaxy Pirates* was on every morning at six. The name had nothing to do with the song by The Rolling Stones.

"OK, Jack Flash. Do you want to play on the swings?"

"No, sir. I can only walk around the path. The playground is dangerous, and I might get hurt. Mommy says so."

"Please don't call me sir. My name is Cyrus. Do I look like your mother?"

Jack giggled, "no, silly. You're a boy."

"So, if you're mother isn't here, how is she going to know? Look, Jack. When you're with Cyrus, Jack Flash can do whatever he feels like doing. Jeremiah can't play on the swings. Jack Flash can. Got it?"

"Yes, Cyrus. But what if she finds out?"

"How's she going to find out? The answer is she won't. You just have to remember to become Jeremiah again at home."

"I know." Jack smiled up at me, took my hand, and we ran for the swings.

CHAPTER FOUR

S ome of the lessons I picked up at school, plus my own experiences traveling around the city led me to a core belief that one should know their surroundings. According to my social studies teacher, most cities were set up the same way. I lived in the preppy or yuppie area where people acted as if their crap didn't stink. Many of my neighbors had faces that might only be replicated by inserting an icicle up their ass.

Downtown was the main drag where the denizens of the other areas congregated to conduct business, shop, and intermingle for a brief time. Petula Clark wrote an old song about such an area.

One might find a few ethnic enclaves if the city was big enough. Some of these sections also crossed over with what were termed the bad sections of town. The areas termed bad were where the drug dealers hung out. Such enclaves were where one might find adult stores and dance clubs in which only the ladies danced. One would also find people who fenced stolen property, and other undesirable elements in these areas. Another popular term for this area was a ghetto.

The park where I hung out with Jack Flash was a microcosm of the macrocosm. There was no business as such, unless one included the food carts, and occasional purveyors of balloons, gimcracks, and gewgaws. The main section, akin to downtown, was the playground. To the east was a wooded area where the rougher element hung out. Drugs were peddled, and stolen merchandise was swapped or sold. To the west were the gardens which attracted the snobby, nose-in-the-air crowds.

There was even an ethnic area of sorts. Benches were set up on the far side of the playground, and there were tables with built in checkers and chess boards. Older Jewish men, and older African American men would sit in that area and play checkers, chess, and dominoes. They'd also shout at each other and banter about the local news stories.

As with any town, the park had multitudes of bag ladies and homeless men who crossed all the sections. These people slept where they could, scavenged the trash receptacles, and were met with varying degrees of acceptance by others. I never interacted with them, but neither did I have anything against them.

I stood up from the swings and spread my arms toward the entire park. "Jack, my friend, this is our little piece of turf. We must know it well so that we can avoid the bad guys. Now then, the bad guys aren't who you might think Your mother may think certain people are bad guys who are actually good guys. She doesn't know as much as she thinks she does. Understand?"

"Yes, Cyrus. I know that sometimes Mommy pulls me away when I'm talking to nice people. Like those men on the benches over there. She says that they aren't our kind. I don't know why. They're always friendly to me."

"Exactly." I thought to myself what a narrow-minded, racist, Neo-Nazi piece of garbage Ms. Cramer was. "When you come to the park with her, you're Jeremiah. You do what she says.

With Cyrus you're Jack Flash and the bad guys aren't the same. Got it?"

"I guess so." He shrugged.

We walked along the garden path, and Jack looked to be mulling over the information I had just imparted. All of a sudden, something smashed against his head. It was a large leather handbag, and it was attached to the arm of a moderately overweight African American bag lady with sagging skin, and a bushy afro flecked with grey. She'd been swinging her bag and hadn't even noticed Jack standing there.

I looked down and Jack was rubbing his head but not crying. I turned my gaze on the lady and glared. "Hey! Watch it with the damned purse, lady! You could have concussed the kid!"

"Then you watch where you're walking. You're blocking up the entire path, young man."

Jack and I kept walking. I stopped after a few paces and knelt down. "You OK, buddy?"

Jack smiled a toothy grin. "I'm OK. Was she one of the bad guys?"

I shook my head, "She's one of the good guys. She just needs to watch where she's going."

I lifted Jack into my arms and then put him on my shoulders. We kept moving through the garden area, checking out the flora and fauna. We stopped at a bench, and I lowered Jack to the ground.

"This is our hangout for now. We have to sit here and keep watch on the area. Make sure no bad guys show up."

I sat and began sketching a large bush. Jack asked for some paper and a pencil. I delivered, and he began sketching as well. He wasn't half bad for a five-year-old. On the bench across from us a man sat down and extracted a harmonica. He was large around the waist and had a beard and mustache. Beside him sat a well-behaved dog. If I hadn't known it was impossible, I'd have sworn that the dog was conversing with the man.

"Hey, Swee'Pea, do you think that this is a good spot to attract a paying crowd?" The man asked.

The dog nodded and appeared to agree that the spot would do.

The man began blowing a tune and I found myself absorbed in the music. Jack was similarly enraptured. We stopped sketching and listened. The man played for ten minutes and then took a rest.

"That was 'Blue Midnight' by Little Walter. My name is James, but most call me Get Lost Jimmy. It's a long story why."

I tossed two dollars at the man's feet. "I'm Cyrus Ahriman. This is Jack Flash."

"Pleasure to meet you. My son here is Swee'Pea."

Jack leaned down to pet the dog and was rewarded with a few kisses. "He's a very nice dog, mister." Jack smiled. "Do you know Jimmy Cracked Corn?"

Get Lost Jimmy began to play, and Jack started to sing and dance. A crowd gathered and threw change and a few bills. I collected the money as the duo performed. For an encore they performed "I've Been Working on The Railroad."

After they finished, I handed the money to Jimmy. "That was amazing. I didn't know Jack could sing and dance that well."

"He your brother?"

"No, sir. Just a kid for whom I babysit. More like I get paid to hang out with him. He isn't a baby, and he doesn't do much sitting."

Get Lost Jimmy chuckled. "Well, it was enjoyable. I think I'll just sit here and meditate a while with my son."

Jack and I walked away and continued to a spot where the path looped back on itself. We sat on another bench and began sketching a different tree. Another man approached and sat across from us. He had a close-cropped haircut and was enormous both circumferentially and lengthwise. He wasn't obese in a slovenly way, but rather was rotund the way that Lou Costello of Abbot and Costello was.

The man's attire was worthy of notice. He had on a pink leisure suit, a pink dress shirt, and a red checkered bowtie. On his feet were saddle shoes, and on his face the thickest pair of glasses I had ever seen. He looked somewhere between a nerd in an old college movie, and The Hindenburg. Jack giggled, and I elbowed him to hush.

After my initial shock at the man's attire, I noticed a majestic aura about him. He was large but dignified. He also appeared oblivious to our stares. After the enjoyable encounter with Get Lost Jimmy, I decided that we should introduce ourselves to this man as well.

"Excuse me, sir. I was about to purchase lunch for myself and my friend here, would you care for anything?" I tried to sound natural.

"Certainly. That would be quite nice." The man replied in a dignified tone. "I'm not a vagrant, you understand. I just enjoy this spot to people watch."

"I wasn't suggesting that. I just thought it would be a nice gesture." I took Jack by the hand.

The man led the way, and we approached a vendor's cart. I ordered Six Chicago style dogs, five all the way and one without the peppers. Jack and I chose grape sodas with our meal. I handed our new friend three of the hotdogs and took two for myself. Jack got the one without the sport pepper.

The man took a bite of his first Chicago dog, and a gulp of soda. "A pleasure to have company for lunch. People call me Uncle Don. And you are?"

"I'm Cyrus Ahriman."

"I'm Jack Flash."

"My pleasure to know you Cyrus, Jack." We ate in silence for a few moments. "I used to be a wood carver and a sculptor in my early days. It was quite a time in this area. Art studios abounded."

We sat and listened to Uncle Don regale us with tales of his youthful forays, and with information about the lost art of wood carving. As we listened and he chatted, the elderly lady from earlier walked by. She noticed our hotdogs and muttered to herself.

"Hotdogs. I can't stand them. Give me a good bratwurst any day, but not a hotdog. My father used to make a bratwurst that had people coming from miles around. They were to die for. Now, nobody wants anything but hotdogs. The vendors refuse to even carry bratwurst. It isn't fair. No consideration for those who live in this park." The lady shuffled along muttering angrily.

"What is she carrying on about?" I asked Uncle Don and pulled Jack a bit closer to me.

"Well, it appears that she prefers bratwurst to hotdogs. I must say that she has a point, however I do also enjoy many varieties of sandwich along those lines."

"A hotdog is a hotdog, isn't it? I mean other than the toppings." I finished my last bite and drank down my last swallow.

Jack burped and giggled. "What's the difference?" He leaned on me and yawned a bit.

"Hotdogs and bratwurst are both types of sausages. They are both served on a bread bun, and both are tasty. However, they are not the same." Uncle Don explained. "Bratwurst is a type of German sausage that is commonly made with pork, beef or veal and seasoned with ginger, nutmeg, coriander, lemon zest or caraway. The first documented evidence of bratwurst dates back to the early 1300s, in Nuremberg, Germany. Brats aren't finely ground like hotdogs. They have a course and heavy texture. Usually, they come raw and must be grilled before consuming, lest one become ill."

"They sound delicious." I said.

"Delicious." Jack yawned.

Uncle Don continued, "Hotdogs also have their roots in Germany. Hence the term frankfurter. Despite those German origins, the hotdog was made popular in the United States in the early 1900s, when it became a working-class street food sold by cart vendors.

So, how do hotdogs differ from bratwurst? In general, they're more processed than bratwurst and may contain more sodium and preservatives. Hotdog meat is emulsified into a paste, so it has a very smooth texture. Unlike the brat, they're cooked during manufacture and can be eaten without additional preparation, although they are usually warmed before serving."

"I see." I moved Jack onto my lap so he could nap.

"The lady is correct. About ten years ago they had a bratwurst stand here in the park. However, sales were slow, and more people purchased hotdogs. I was disappointed myself at the turn of events, but the laws of economics hold out."

Uncle Don finished his food, thanked me, and stood up. As he walked away, I sat holding Jack in my lap and watching people go by. There was a good blend of nationalities in the area, tourists and otherwise. I saw several females with whom I would have enjoyed spending time, or at least with whom I would have enjoyed making time.

An hour later Jack woke up refreshed and full of pep. The sound of a guitar and a harmonica broke through the near silence of the afternoon. Jack and I walked along the path and, under a tree, spotted a man in his twenties playing an acoustic guitar. He had hair to his shoulders, a goatee, and was dressed in a flannel shirt with the sleeves ripped off, jeans, combat boots, and an orange baseball cap. He was playing a bluesy riff, and Get Lost Jimmy was jamming with him on harmonica.

Uncle Don appeared, and so did several of the homeless denizens of the park. The guitarist began singing a song about someone named Momo and about black cats. It was a pretty tune, and I looked down to see Jack rocking back and forth to it. When the song finished, the guitarist noticed Jack and began to play a familiar tune. Jack and I harmonized on the theme to The Flintstones. A man in a suit walked by and dropped cash into the open guitar case.

"Hey dudes, like s'up?" The guitarist was chilled out and mellow. "You dudes made me some money and that's out of sight, man. The name is Top Cat, dudes. Who are you?"

I introduced myself and Jack. Uncle Don approached and introduced himself. We stated that we knew Jimmy and Swee'Pea. It turned out that Uncle Don had seen them numerous times as well.

"Thanks for the do-re-mi, dudes. Be seeing you around?" Top Cat began putting his instrument away.

"Jack and I come here daily." I said. It was technically our first foray, but I planned to continue.

"You're quite the performer," Uncle Don stated to Top Cat.

"Do you perform any classical guitar? I have connections at WTLK and could put in a good word for you. Assuming you have any interest in performing on the radio."

"Sure, man. I can play anything on this ax of mine. Radio sounds amazingly great, and I'm for certain that it would top throw change in the park."

"I'll see what I can arrange," Uncle Don said. "The station is on strike at the moment, but in time management will give in to the demands of labor. Once that occurs, I will see what can be done."

Uncle Don handed Top Cat a business card, and handed one to me, Jack, and Jimmy as well. It read: Donald M. Schmaltzburger: Talent Agent and Asst. Musical Director WTLK. I placed my card and Jack's in my shirt pocket.

"Hey, let's do lunch tomorrow, my treat." Top Cat lifted his instrument and grabbed his sack. "You dudes made me some cash, and Don here is hooking me up with a professional gig. Least I can do."

I grinned, "Sounds good. We'll see you tomorrow. I need to get this kid home before his mother begins to wonder where we are."

On the way home we stopped at a traffic light, and I knelt down. "Hey, Jack, time to turn back into Jeremiah." I reminded him.

"Yes, sir," He nodded and put his sweater back on. "What we did today was secret. I won't tell about it. Mommy wouldn't understand."

"You got it, Jeremiah." I was secretly amazed at how perceptive he was.

We returned to his house, and I knocked on the door. Ms. Cramer appeared and motioned her son inside.

"Thank you for sitting. Here's forty dollars. Did you enjoy yourselves?"

"Yes, we certainly did. The gardens are simply lovely this time of year." I placed the money neatly in my wallet, shook her hand, and departed.

CHAPTER FIVE

T he next day Jack and I left early in the day to venture toward the park. Ms. Cramer was having her house cleaned, she informed me, and asked if I could be enticed to take her son to the park earlier for an extra $20.00.

I despised people who believed that they could make people do their bidding by waving cash around. On the other hand, money was money. I always needed extra, and art supplies weren't cheap. I would have been glad to take Jack early for the usual price, but if the uptight materfamilias wanted to pad my wallet, I saw no reason to decline the offer.

When Jack and I were two blocks away, I removed his sweater and stuffed it into my knapsack. "And with the removal of your sweater, we change you from Jeremiah into Jack Flash." I intoned solemnly.

Jack giggled, "But no telling Mommy."

We walked by a corner deli and stopped inside. The place had a delightful aroma, a mingling of spices, meats, cheeses, and pastry. I perused the glass enclosed counter.

"Have you ever had a knish, Jack?"

"What's a knish, Cyrus? I don't think so." He smiled up at me.

"It's a fried pastry stuffed with mashed potatoes, onion, and cheese. Jewish soul food." I ordered two of them and two chocolate egg creams.

"This is yummy." Jack bit into his knish.

"I could eat knish all day," I said, and took another bite of mine. "Ashkenazi immigrants brought knishes to the United States at the turn of the century. I read an article about it once. Knish is a Yiddish word of Slavic origin, related to the Ukrainian knysh and Polish knysz."

Jack burped and then looked across the table at me. "You're smart. I wish I was."

I took a sip of egg cream. "You're pretty smart yourself. You're only five. If you study, and read a lot, you'll learn things."

"This drink is yummy. Mommy doesn't let me have stuff like this. Is it really made with eggs?"

I chuckled, "Nah. It's milk, soda water, and chocolate syrup. No eggs or cream involved."

"Then why do they call it that? It's a silly name." Jack burped and finished his drink.

"Not so silly if you know the history. It's another Jewish soul food delicacy. Some say that the term egg is a corruption of the Yiddish echt which means genuine or real. So, an egg cream is a good creamy drink."

"Oh. Now I know about knish, egg cream, and bratwurst. I have stuff to share at show and tell." Jack smiled.

"Remember, you have to be Jeremiah when we aren't to-gether."

"I know. I can just say I heard about it from someone."

As we were leaving, Uncle Don walked in. "Hello, my young friends," He sounded jovial. "How are you this fine morning."

"Doing fine," I shrugged. "We just finished breakfast. Heading to the park now."

Jack looked up and gave a shy smile. He looked away, and his face registered angst. I knelt down.

"Something wrong?"

"Yeah. I forgot about those people yesterday. It isn't fair."

Uncle Don walked to the counter and ordered a blueberry muffin and a hot chocolate. "Would you two care to join me? I'll get you each a cocoa."

Jack nodded. I returned to our table. "Thanks. Much appreciated."

We sat sipping hot chocolates when Uncle Don cleared his throat. "You were saying something isn't fair? What isn't?"

"That lady yesterday with the big purse. She wanted one of those bratwursts. I saw other ladies with bags, too. And there were men sleeping on the benches or pushing carts. I bet they'd like to have bratwurst. Nobody asks them, though. Nobody cares what they want. Nobody cares what I want, either. I'm just a little kid and have to do what people tell me." Jack sounded somewhere between anger and tears.

I patted his shoulder. "It's OK, buddy. That's just the way things are in this lousy country."

Jack shook his head. "It isn't OK. I would have been nice to that lady even if she did bonk me with her bag. I'd be nice to all those people. They look like they need friends. No one asks me, though. They say I'm five and so I have to do what I'm told. If I ask why, or argue, I get smacked. You're the only one who treats me like a big boy, Cyrus. Mommy tells me to be a big boy, and then she treats me like a baby."

I took a moment to ponder what Jack had just said. For a kid he was deep and perceptive. "Hey, look. With me you can be a big kid. You are a big kid. I understand. I really do. I was five once. Thing of it is adults are jerks. Our nation sucks. We can't do much about it."

Uncle Don gave me a stern look. "You shouldn't generalize so much, young man. Some adults do care. I care a great deal about the transient population in the park. I have been thinking since yesterday about them, as a matter of fact."

I sneered, "Oh yeah? What about them?"

"Perhaps," Uncle Don said with a smile, "if we gathered them together and held a small picket line, we could get a return of the bratwursts."

"That sounds cool. Sure. Let's do it." I looked at Uncle Don with a new respect.

"What's a picket line?" Jack asked.

"Well, my young friend," Uncle Don said, "it's when a group of people march around in a circle with signs expressing their dissatisfaction with the established order."

"Does anyone care? Does anyone listen to them?" Jack asked.

"They do, eventually. I was recently involved in a picket at my place of employment. Management behaves in an unfair manner and refuses to provide proper remuneration in comparison to the work provided by the employees."

Jack looked puzzled. I ruffled his hair. "His boss doesn't pay him enough money."

"That is correct." Uncle Don nodded and cleared our paper cups and wrappers from the table. "I for one work very long hours, but management doesn't wish to offer me a higher salary or overtime. I stopped picketing because the behavior of some of my colleagues became distasteful to the point of being frightening. I don't dare return to work, however, until the strike is over."

"Uncle Don, where do you work?" I inquired as Jack, and I

stood.

Uncle Don raised himself from his chair, "I work two counties over. At the radio station listed on the business card I gave you. I have a summer home in this town, and I decided to make use of it." He opened the door for us, "So is the picket line agreed upon?"

"It sounds like a fine idea. I'm an artist, and so is Jack. We can create some signs for the protest, but I'm uncertain how we get the interested parties together and involved."

Uncle Don shrugged, "leave that part to me."

We left the bakery and began walking toward the park. Once we reached the path it occurred to me that Uncle Don still hadn't said much about his career. He didn't seem inclined to discuss his life outside of the park. Up ahead we saw Top Cat having a chat with a homeless lady.

"Hey, Top Cat. How are things?" I asked.

"Oh, howdy dude man. I was just chatting with my friend Hetty here." He introduced us, and hands were shaken all around. It was the same lady who had bonked Jack with her purse.

"I am terribly sorry about yesterday. If I'd known that you were friends with Top Cat, I wouldn't have been so rude."

Jack nodded up at her, and I brushed the matter away. It was, to my thinking, a pathetic reason to be nice to someone or not based upon whom that someone knew We strolled along further, and Jack began running toward the playground.

I followed him toward the swing-sets as Uncle Don took a seat on his bench. Top Cat sat beneath a tree and began playing his guitar. Hetty continued onward pushing a cart. I watched Jack swing and sketched a picture of an oak tree. As I sketched a poem came to me. It wasn't a great poem but being my first I felt that it had some merit. It was based on an old tree house that my friends and I used as a fort when we were Jack's age.

Tree House
Nothing left now but
boards and pieces of ruined tree with
nails thrusting out.
Monument to the steel invasion.
I once stood up there on high
where now there is nothing.
Could I have been so high,
no cares at all?
I tried growing up, to be an adult.
Now, with my feet firmly planted on the ground,
I wish I was up on high once more.
In my old tree house.

I didn't understand any deeper implications in my work, but that evening at class Mr. K informed me that the poem represented the struggle between my ego and my id. He stated that it was natural for a fifteen-year-old to feel such conflict, and that he was impressed by my work.

After I finished my drawing and poem, Jack Flash jumped off the swings and walked over. "Hey, Cyrus. Can we go sit with Uncle Don again? He's a good guy."

We approached the bench where Uncle Don appeared to be deep in thought. I sat beside him, and Jack sat beside me. Fifteen minutes later Top Cat approached with his guitar case slung across his back and carrying a container with hotdogs, a bag of corn chips, and Cokes. He handed me two hotdogs with everything, handed Jack one, and handed Uncle Don two. He kept two for himself.

"Thank you, TC," I spoke around a mouthful of hotdog. I took a swig of my Coke, swallowed, and belched. "I was wondering something. Do you think that if we spoke to Hetty, you think she might be able to get the other homeless people organized?"

Top Cat stopped mid-bite. "Organized for what, dude?" He resumed eating.

"If we can get all the people who live in the park to organize a picket line, we can picket the hotdog vendor to bring back bratwursts? Hetty prefers them to hotdogs, and she said that most of the others do as well."

"Huh? What are you talking about?" Top Cat tilted his head and gave me a look.

Uncle Don patted his mouth with a handkerchief. "The idea is that our young friends will arrange signs and other matters necessary for a protest. We gather the bag ladies, the homeless men, and any others who show interest. Together we march to the vendor and demand that he resumes sales of bratwursts. If necessary, Hetty and her friends can make a small scene. The end result is that they get noticed, and the vendor must negotiate."

"Excellent, dude. That's a brilliant scheme. I'll join in the marching, although I don't care for bratwurst myself. I understand that they used to be popular, and I would guess that size-wise they provide more bang for the buck."

Jack bounced around where he sat. "That's very nice of you. This is going to be fun."

Top Cat looked at me and Jack. "Might not look like it, but I know what it is to live on a fixed income. I reside in a Volkswagen that's parked down the street. I'm two shakes and a shimmy from living on the benches and in the bushes like the others, dudes."

Jack looked serious, and I shook my head feeling sad. "I didn't know that" I said. "If you need anything, let me know. I can bring you shampoo, soap, whatever. Probably can get you a couple of blankets as well."

Top Cat nodded, "I'm good. If I need anything I'll let you know. So, back to this protest thing. Would Saturday be too soon? I think I could have the people ready to march by then."

We agreed, and hands were shook all around. Top Cat threw the remains of our meal into a trash receptacle and tuned up his guitar. He began to play a song about Jamaica, and Uncle Don joined in with the singing. Someone threw a dollar into the guitar case.

"Mr. Top Cat," Jack asked, "Do you know any songs for people my age?"

"Sure, dude." Top Cat began to play a series of songs for children, and Jack Flash sang along. An hour later they had collected a bunch of bills. Top Cat put his guitar away. "That's the best I've made in several weeks. The crowds like you, little dude."

"I'm not that little," Jack pouted and then giggled. "Well, maybe next to you I'm a lot shorter."

CHAPTER SIX

At three in the afternoon, I took Jack home. He entered and removed his sweater hanging it up neatly. Ms. Cramer held up a hand for me to wait a moment.

"Jeremiah, please go get washed up, and read quietly in your room. I need to speak with Cyrus." Jack walked up the stairs, and I stood waiting. "I received word that there is an emergency meeting of a company in which I own stock. I realize that this is impossibly short notice, but could you be persuaded to spend the night here? I'd offer you $100.00."

"That sounds fine, ma'am." I nodded politely, "I would need to return home and let the housekeeper know. Also, I would need to get some things from my house. I could return by five."

"That would be fine. I shall expect you then."

I left and dashed home. One hundred dollars for hanging out all night sounded like an insane amount of money to me. I was glad to take the cash, though. I entered my house and saw that my mother was in the living room.

"Mother, Ms. Cramer asked me to babysit overnight. I said that it would be OK. She's paying me well for this." I waited for the response.

She frowned at me and sighed. "I suppose it has to be OK, then. I can't imagine why she thinks this is a good idea. You don't even have the consideration to ask your father or me before accepting such an offer. What if we needed you here?" My mother stood and glared at me. "You never keep your room clean or show the slightest interest in anything practical. How you care for a child is beyond me. Why anyone would trust you to care for a child is beyond me." She began pacing as she lectured me. "At least you're showing some interest in the capitalist process. I figured with your art classes, that garbage you call music, and the fact that you do so poorly in math and science, you were either a homo or a communist. I suppose if you're making money at a job then that's something. I still don't know why you didn't want to be an office assistant at your father's firm. You could get life experience for your future." My mother finished ranting at me and sat again.

"Yes, Mother. Thank you for allowing me to take this job. I'll tidy up my room before I depart." I said. "*I'll be sure to give Comrades Lenin and Marx your regards,*" I thought to myself.

I stopped in the kitchen and put a frozen pizza into the oven for my dinner. While it cooked, I went upstairs and organized my room. I made the bed with hospital corners, dusted, and straightened up my art supplies and books. I returned to the kitchen and was eating when my father entered.

"Heard you picked up a promotion."

I shrugged, "I suppose it is. I was asked to babysit overnight. I apologize for not asking first. I cleaned my room."

My father reached into the refrigerator and took out a Heineken. "It's fine. I told her to keep her mouth shut. You're working. You're making good money for little effort. I wish you had accepted the internship at my office, but I guess I can't expect miracles. At least you're making your own money."

I said nothing. The last part of his speech said enough. One might suspect that my father was proud of me, but that would never be the case. I was never going to be good enough for him unless I became a lawyer, or a high-priced executive corporate raider. He wanted me to be a Rush Limbaugh quoting, Bob Grant following, conservative. The only part of my job that he cared about was that I had my own money, so I didn't have to ask him for any.

After finishing my pizza, drowned with a quart of milk, I rinsed my dishes and put them into the dishwasher. I returned to my room and changed into BDU pants, a black t-shirt, a leather jacket, and combat boots. I donned fingerless biker gloves with studs on them, and a black leather fedora. I removed $75.00 from the miniature safe on my desk, filled my wallet, and left.

I dashed back to The Cramer's and knocked. Jack looked through a curtain, and then unlocked the door. He was watching cartoons.

"Mommy left already. She said there's an envelope on the counter with a key in it and money." Jack looked up at me.

I reached down and scooped him up. "And Cyrus scoops Jack Flash for the big body slam!" I gently dropped him on the soft couch cushions.

"Cyrus, why are you dressed in that costume?" Jack giggled.

I did my best impression of Top Cat, "Yeah, dude. We're like going on an adventure tonight. All night movies, man!" I laughed.

"I'm not allowed to stay up all night."

"Your mother isn't home. She won't be back until tomorrow around three. How's she to know?"

"My bedtime is eight. Eight-thirty sometimes, but no books before bed." Jack stated as if by remote.

"F...orget that noise, Jack! Do I look like your mother? I'm in charge tonight, and I say you can do as you please."

"No, you don't look like Mommy. You're a boy, silly." Jack laughed. "I have more fun with you, too."

"Jack Flash, my friend, you can do whatever you want to tonight. If you fall asleep at the movies, don't worry either. You can sleep in my lap."

"That sounds like fun. What movie are we seeing?"

"There's a triple feature. *The Warriors*, *Over the Edge*, and *Times Square*. They're great movies." I walked to the kitchen, pocketed the key ring and the cash, and checked the refrigerator. There was, naturally, no soda pop, no junk food, and nothing worth giving to a child. I poured myself a glass of water from the dispenser in the front of the door.

"When do we go to the movies?" Jack came looking for me.

"In about 4 hours. We'll stop for a snack first, and then head over."

I took my water and headed back to the living room with Jack. We settled on the couch to watch Wheel of Fortune. Jack leaned against me.

"Hey, Jack? Where does your mother hide the good food? All I see in the kitchen is Styrofoam discs, bee spit, plain yoghurt, and a lot of vegetables."

He giggled. "Those are rice cakes. And I don't think we eat bee spit."

"That greenish-yellow goo."

"Oh. That's kale and squash yoghurt dip for the rice cakes."

I made a face. "You like eating that sh...tuff?"

"I have to. Mommy gets mad if I don't eat what she gives me. I like what you give me better, though. But I know, no telling her about that."

41

We sat and watched the rest of the game show before deciding that Jack needed an outfit for the movies. We looked through his dresser, and I found an old pair of jeans that had some fraying at the knees. He had a worn-out tie-dyed t-shirt under a pile of designer shirts, and we found a baseball cap in his closet that said "Ride or Die" on it.

"I'm surprised your mother lets you have a hat like this." I took it off the shelf.

"I'm not allowed to wear it. An uncle gave it to me, from my daddy's side. Before he left us. He gave me that t-shirt too. I think that's an oak leaf on it."

I double checked the image on the t-shirt, and it was indeed a leaf. The leaf wasn't oak, however, and I decided not to say anything about it. "Well, let's get you washed up and dressed, Jack Flash."

"OK." He led the way to the bathroom.

As I ran the tub, Jack undressed. I instantly sensed something was wrong, although I didn't put everything together at that time. When Jack was getting into the tub, I noticed some purplish-black bruising on his buttocks, some greyish-green bruises on his thighs, and some bruising on his lower back. He also had an oblong bruise on his chest that was fading.

"What happened, Jack? That looks like it hurts."

"I...I fell down the stairs the other day. Mommy says I'm clumsy."

I nodded and dismissed the situation. Looking under the sink I found a bottle of bubble bath. I added it to the water. Jack gasped.

"That isn't mine. That's for mommy and her boyfriend. I'm not allowed to touch it. Baths are for getting clean quickly and getting dried off fast." Jack looked up at me.

"I'll make sure I buy a new bottle on the way home tonight. I didn't know, sorry." I shook my head and tried to swallow my irritation with Ms. Cramer. The woman took any enjoyment out of her son's life. I also had a gnawing sense of discomfort with Jack's explanation about his bruises.

"You mad at me, Cyrus? Did I do something bad?" Jack looked as if he might cry.

"Nah. Nothing's wrong." I smiled and scooped bubbles to make a beard for Jack.

He soaked in the tub and played with the bubbles for a while. Afterward I dried him off and put some arnica ointment on his bruises. "You're gonna look great in this outfit, buddy." I helped him dress.

Jack looked like a miniature biker, and I completed the look by taking one of my bandanas and tying it on him as a neckerchief. We found a pair of hiking boots in his closet, and I helped him tie them. After we walked downstairs, I turned off the TV.

"If you want, we can go early. Maybe we can walk through the park before the movies." I hoisted Jack onto my back and gave him a piggyback ride.

As we walked through the neighborhood, and into the main thoroughfare, I looked around at the night sky and the lit-up buildings. The city had a beauty to it, a sort of insalubrious charm that was difficult for me to articulate. I knew instinctively that I would need to bring my sketchpad one evening and draw what I was seeing.

Jack and I walked to the park and found a bench. There were more homeless people than usual walking the paths and stopping to chat with friends and acquaintances. A congregation of teenaged males with shaved heads, dressed in undershirts, brown military style pants, black suspenders, and combat boots walked by. I noticed that most were armed with knives or some form of club. The guys were accompanied by female teens who had shaved the crown and back of their heads to about an eighth of an inch. In the front they wore thick bangs, swept to the side with curlicue locks hanging over their temples. A few of the females adorned themselves with nose rings in their septum reminiscent of a bull. Their thin white blouses revealed black brassieres, and they wore plaid skirts and calf-high lace-up boots. As with the males, the females were armed.

I shifted Jack to my lap and watched the miniature army walk by. Something about them didn't sit right with me, but I decided that maybe I was being judgmental. As I held Jack in my lap, I began wondering if it was a good idea to have a five-year-old out at such a late hour. I considered the movies we were heading to see and if they were appropriate for a boy of his age. In the end I realized that when I was five, I never felt as if I was allowed to do anything that big kids got to do. Jack had mentioned to me that he felt as if people expected him to behave like a "big boy," and then treated him like a baby. That was enough reason for me to see our plan through.

"I'm hungry, Cyrus." Jack interrupted my reverie. "Can we get something to eat, and see the movies now?"

"We can go find somewhere to grab a bite, Jack." I smiled. "The movies don't start until later. I don't know if you've ever been to this theater or not. It's off on a side street near downtown. They show double or triple features of older movies, and it's only three dollars to get in. I go sometimes during the day, but usually I don't go out this late to see them."

"Your mommy and daddy don't want you staying up late either?"

"My mother and father don't give a...they don't care, except

44

that it's bad for their image if I'm running around at night like the lower classes."

Jack stood. "What's the lower classes?"

"It's their word for those dudes and chicks we just saw, and for these other people in the park. My parents think they're better than these people. I don't agree."

"Those boys and girls with the bald heads scared me. I shot them with my Jack Flash lasers. They're bad guys."

I shook my head. "They aren't bad guys. At least I don't believe so. I don't really know. I think maybe they're just misunderstood. Doesn't mean I want to tangle with them, or that I plan to army through their turf. They probably aren't bad though. Most likely they just want to be left alone. Like you and me."

CHAPTER SEVEN

J ack and I entered a deli across the street from the movie theater. The place was designed with black and white checkerboard floor tiles, and red paint on the walls. In the corner was a juke box, and behind the counter was a handwritten menu.

"What sounds good to you, Jack?" I looked down at him.

"I've never been here before. What are you having?"

"I'm getting a cup of coffee and some cherry Danish."

"Then that's what I want, too."

I smiled at the server who was a tall blonde, probably college aged and had curves in just the right places. "I'll take a coffee, two creams no sugar, and a Danish. He'll take a hot milk with a shot of coffee in it, and a Danish."

We sat and waited for our order. As we waited, Jack discussed various subjects that appealed to him. Apparently, it was his uncle who had introduced him to cartoons and to Jack Flash. His mother went along with it because it kept him out of her way while she was busy with men that Jack said worked for her and her boyfriend.

I had just taken a bite of my pastry and a sip of coffee when the door to the place opened. In walked Uncle Don. He was dressed more casually than I had seen him previously. He noticed us and pulled up a chair.

"Hello, my young friends. Fancy seeing you both out at this hour. I see you have discovered the best deli in town. I come here frequently before the evening show." Uncle Don shook our hands.

"Hi, Uncle Don." Jack smiled.

Uncle Don excused himself and approached the counter. He returned after a few minutes with a pastrami on rye, three pickle spears, and a small tub of coleslaw. "I always enjoy a snack in the evening."

The three of us sat eating, and at one point Uncle Don bought me a second coffee. We discussed the plans for the upcoming protest. I felt a surge of emotion. It might only have been a protest about bratwurst, but it was the principal of the matter. Society sucked the enjoyment out of poor people's lives. My parents did their best to suck the enjoyment out of mine. I couldn't do anything about my parents, but I could do something about this.

We also discussed the art classes I took during the summer. Uncle Don was acquainted with the works of many famous artists, and I learned a great deal about Modigliani and Brancusi. I took mental notes to use as launching points for discussions in class.

Jack was yawning by the time we approached the theater. I paid for him and myself, and we entered with Uncle Don behind us. We took a seat behind a man dressed in a tuxedo complete with white gloves and a bowler. He was sitting making out with his date, a young, perky redhead.

Before *The Warriors* even started, Jack had climbed into my lap and was asleep. I held him and watched the opening credits roll. It felt strange, almost like I had a child of my own. The situation was comforting in an odd way. I wasn't sure why the thought of having my own child was a comfort, except that I was certain I could do a better job of raising a kid than my parents – or Jack's mother. At least I was giving Jack some pleasure in life instead of constant rules.

The Warriors was a great movie as always. In between that and *Over the Edge*, Uncle Don bought me a Coke. We sat talking quietly as the audience waited for the second film.

"You may not be aware," Uncle Don said, "*Over the Edge* was the first movie that Matt Dillon ever made. In fact, the directors hired an entire cast of unknown and untested teenagers for the film. The movie didn't get much attention at first, because movie theaters were afraid to run it. There were riots and numerous fights in theaters when *The Warriors* was presented, and that led the theaters to be gun shy about *Over the Edge*."

I listened attentively. "That's interesting. I wonder if that's why *Times Square* didn't perform as well, either."

Uncle Don nodded. "That may have been one reason. However, in the case of that movie there were other issues at play. Originally, *Times Square* contained lesbian content which was removed from the final cut. There was also the addition of several songs to the film's soundtrack that didn't work as well with the general theme. It is considered by critics that the producers wanted to rival *Saturday Night Fever* in popularity, but the storyline didn't lend itself to that type of film.

I personally feel that the loss of key lesbian scenes between the main characters left the narrative disjointed and damaged the story's emotion and characterizations. In all it could have been a sensation if the producers had left the story alone."

I listened carefully and took mental notes. Something about Uncle Don reminded me of Mr. K. They were both solid teachers, and they had a way of explaining matters that made sense. I was impressed that Uncle Don didn't feel that there was anything wrong with being a lesbian. I agreed. Love was love and the world needed more of it in every flavor.

Over The Edge started and I made a mental note to investigate the story at the library. The opening credits indicated that the movie was based on true events. I held Jack in my lap as I watched. The movie had an interesting vibe, different than *The Warriors*, but with the same hard edges. I thought about what Uncle Don had told me and noticed where both movies might lend themselves to rioting if the audience was in such a head space.

After the final scene, Jack woke up startled. He looked up at me and calmed down. "Hey, Cyrus, is there a potty here?"

"Sure, Jack." I carried him to the restroom where there was a line of people waiting. We managed to get in and return before *Times Square* commenced.

Uncle Don handed me two cups of Coke. "Here, I bought these for you. I thought you might be thirsty."

"Thank you. You didn't need to do that."

"My pleasure."

Jack sat sipping his soda pop and watching the movie. I made mental notes comparing the storylines of the three films. Of the three, *Times Square* was the least angry in tone. It had a very raw feel to it, though. I had never known anyone like one of the characters, played by Robin Johnson, but the one played by Trini Alvarado reminded me of my own life. She was from an upper middle-class environment and wasn't especially happy with it. I could relate to her feelings and needs.

It was going on three in the morning when the final film ended. Jack was sound asleep on my lap, and I tried not to wake him up as I stood.

"It was an enjoyable evening, Cyrus." Uncle Don stepped into the aisle and yawned. "I hope to see you at the park tomorrow or the next day."

"That's my plan. I need to get this kid home and into his bed. It was nice learning about the movies. Thank you."

I watched the crowds mingling and chatting as I searched for a pay phone. The cab arrived fifteen minutes later, and I took Jack home. He remained asleep when I changed him into pajamas and tucked him in. I crashed on the floor beside his bed.

I woke up at ten in the morning and Jack was already awake. I found him in the living room watching cartoons. He was subdued, but not exhausted.

"Want some pancakes and eggs?" I asked.

"That sounds yummy. I only get pancakes on my birthday. I've never had eggs alone. Mommy says they have too much something in them. It's bad for your heart."

"Cholesterol?"

"Yeah, that."

I searched the kitchen for ingredients and muttered some unmentionable words about Ms. Cramer. She was like a lot of new age trendy people who took the health food kick too far. In fact, there was no white flour in the kitchen and no sugar. I discovered that whole wheat flour and honey can work. The taste wasn't terrible.

After breakfast we got dressed and headed to the park. Top Cat was there playing guitar, and Get Lost Jimmy was backing him up on harmonica. Uncle Don sat listening to them. He had brought some large pieces of colored cardboard and markers to make signs for the protest.

Top Cat started in on a series of songs by Woodie Guthrie, and Get Lost Jimmy really wailed on his mouth-harp. Uncle Don suggested slogans to me, and I wrote them on the boards. Jack drew pictures of hotdogs with a circle around them and a line through the circle. I started to wonder if the protest would really make a difference.

The sky turned dark grey all of a sudden, and we all made a mad dash for a gazebo. As we were taking seats, lightning cracked, and thunder boomed. The downpour was fierce, and we moved toward the center of the gazebo where it was a bit drier.

Uncle Don cleared his throat. "If everyone agrees, we could hold the protest on Saturday at noon."

I looked around at my friends. "I think that we should let the park residents do the marching. Maybe we can direct things from the side. This is their fight after all."

"That sounds good, dude," Top Cat nodded. "I'll join the marchers, though. But, yeah, dude, you guys stay to the side."

Jack looked up at me. "Can I sing Blowing in The Wind? I know that song from school."

"I can even accompany you on my harp." Get Lost Jimmy said.

As the rain let up, we each left our separate ways. I took Jack home and ran a load of laundry. I had his clothes and mine dried before Ms. Cramer returned. Jack was dressed in jeans and a polo shirt, and I was reading to him from *Charlie and The Chocolate Factory*.

"Thank you for watching Jeremiah, Cyrus. I hope he wasn't too much trouble."

"No trouble at all, ma'am. We went to the park today but returned when the clouds grew dark. I didn't wish for your son to catch cold."

Ms. Cramer smiled at my answer and pressed a hundred-dollar bill into my hand. "You are a good babysitter. My meeting went well. Here's an extra bill. I'll call you later to plan about tomorrow."

I put the money into my wallet and walked home. I was just walking inside when the phone rang. It was Dawn Larkspur.

CHAPTER EIGHT

I was not particularly thrilled to be talking to Dawn. She and I attended VHI together, but we moved in different social circles. Dawn hung out with an obnoxious crowd of snobby girls who acted superior to me and other students who operated on the fringes.

Dawn was the daughter of Cassandra Larkspur; the know-nothing child shrink. I had read two books by Dr. Larkspur, had listened to her radio show, and was unimpressed with her views. Dawn, as far as I knew, was formed from the same mold. I hadn't exchanged more than fifty words with her the entire school year, and most of them were obscenities on my part.

The fact remained that most of my peers were vacationing in Europe or attending family gatherings in other states. I had no one my age with whom I could spend time, and as much as I loved Jack, I felt the need to spend time with someone my own age.

Truth be told, Dawn was attractive physically. She had blonde hair that came to her shoulders and framed her face perfectly. She had water-blue eyes, perfect teeth, a dainty nose, and full lips. Her bustline was a perfect c-cup, and from behind I gathered she poured herself into her pants. Molded, man. Absolutely molded.

I held the receiver in my hand and took a deep breath. "Hi. What have you been doing this summer?" I asked.

"Nothing much. Everyone is out of town except us. I was supposed to go on a cruise, but my parents both have conferences to attend, and I can't go alone."

"So, what do you want?" I tried not to sound hostile.

"I was wondering if you wanted to go for a walk?" She said. "I have to get out of my house. I can't take being cooped up anymore."

"Walk where?"

"Anywhere. You name it. I want to talk to you."

"I'll be on the corner of your block in an hour and a half. Be there." I hung up.

I turned and grabbed a carrot stick from a pile Mrs. Ferrigno was inspecting. "How are things? Mind if I have a carrot?"

She smiled. "Help yourself. I'll peel your carrot if you like."

"That's OK." I took a good chomp and walked into the living room. My parents were reading the paper.

"Hello, Mother. Hello, Father. The babysitting is working out well. I'm putting away some money for college."

My mother looked up at me. "That's a good idea, but I wonder if you'll be accepted anywhere. You certainly won't get into one of the better universities with your grades. I'm certain that most schools will be impressed that you have babysitting on your resume. Much better than working as a clerk in an office."

I nodded, "Yes, Mother. Perhaps next summer I will give the office work a try."

My father looked over his newspaper and eyed me. "No need for the sarcasm, young man. We're concerned for your future."

"I appreciate that." I turned and headed upstairs. After a long shower, and a shave, I changed into my "8-ball" t-shirt.

I dug the band. Their lead guitarist was great, and the singer brought a certain guttural je ne sais quoi to his art. I paired the shirt with pants I had purchased at an army-navy store. The pants were supposed to be out of date Marine corps dress slacks, but they looked exactly like some pants I had seen at The Gap. I slipped on a pair of socks and my combat boots.

I put on my earphones and cranked up a tape of El Grande. He was a punk/folk singer that I was getting into. As the music played, I perused a copy of *Hot and Wet* magazine. I was bored. For the first time in a week, I had nothing to do. Between babysitting, evening art classes, the gym, and a few chores my week was filled to capacity.

An hour later I told my parents that I was going for a walk and took off. They had a business function to attend anyway. I walked a few blocks and stood on the corner. Dawn was five minutes late.

I looked her up and down. She was prettier than ever. She was wearing black high-top Chuck Taylor's, skintight jeans that accentuated her curves and folds, and a tight black t-shirt. It was clear that she had opted to forgo a bra. Her blonde hair was silky, and she had put on mascara and lipstick. It occurred to me that she liked me. I mean why would she dress that way if she didn't.

"You're late." I watched her walking towards me, my eyes following her bouncing breasts.

"I lost track of time. Sorry. What do you think would be a suitable punishment?" She giggled.

"Umm..." I was left speechless by her forward comment. "Uh...you look very nice. I was thinking maybe we could walk to the park. I'll get us some ice cream on the way."

Dawn stepped in closer and wrapped her arms around my

waist. She was two inches shorter than me. Before I could react to her hugging me, she lifted her head and kissed me. A deep romantic kiss.

"I've been wanting to do that all year, Francis."

"*Woah, baby! Now what the hell was that about?*" I collected myself quickly and scowled. "The name is Cyrus. I don't go by Francis anymore. Except to my parents.

"Yes, sir, Cyrus. You're in a mood tonight."

"Yeah? Maybe I am. You aren't exactly the girl I know from school. Want to try that kiss again?" I wished I'd worn looser pants so my reaction to her wasn't so visible.

I lowered my head. We kissed each other as instinctively I ran my hands over her tight, denim covered posterior. I held her close, feeling her breasts press against me. My feelings about her from school kept clashing with my feelings of the moment. Her coming on to me was making everything hard.

I pulled away and started walking toward the park. "Let's bounce, girl."

Dawn slipped her hand into mine. "Don't call me, girl. My name is Dawn." She giggled.

I kept looking at her and then looking away. "So, what have you been doing this summer?"

"Dawn shrugged, "I sit in my room watching TV and reading magazines. I'm bored stiff. There's nothing to do."

"*I'm stiff as a board, too.*" I thought to myself.

We entered the park and located an empty bench in a dark area along the path. Dawn leaned her head on my shoulder and sighed. She sat up and looked at me as if searching for words.

"Do you like me, Cyrus?" She asked.

"Yeah, sure. I guess so. I'm a little confused here, but yeah. Yes. Sure, I like you."

"Don't sound so enthusiastic. Why are you confused?"

I looked her in the eyes for a moment, and then looked away. "You don't know? All year long you've been a total snobby bitch to me and my friends. You and that trendy-girl crowd you hang out with. You act like your excrement doesn't stink. Then out of the blue you call me and want to get together. The minute we see each other you're coming on to me. If this is a game you're playing, I'll make sure you pay for it."

Dawn moved away on the bench. "Ouch. I guess I deserve that. I guess saying I'm sorry isn't enough."

"Nope. But I forgive you anyway. Mind if I ask why the change of attitude?"

"Damn, Cyrus. I like you. Most of the girls do. I just...my parents have a standard for me. I have to live up to it. I don't want to, but you have no idea the consequences if I don't. You don't understand the pressure on me."

"I bet I do. I have the same pressure on me. I still don't treat people like I'm superior to them. I also don't give in to the pressure. My father wanted me to work in an office this summer. I decided to take a babysitting job and get college credits by taking an art class taught by Mr. K."

Dawn turned away and when she looked back, she had a few tears dribbling down her cheeks. "What do you want from me? I'm sorry I treated you bad this past year. What? You want I should drop my pants and go across your lap?"

I stammered again, "Ummm...no. Uh, where is that comment coming from?"

Dawn shook her head, "Nothing. Never mind. I...it's nothing. I was at Faith Lumpkin's sweet sixteen and she had some movies hidden in her basement. I...I can't explain."

I laughed, "Not with a mother like yours you can't. I understand just fine. I have my own stash of magazines. I get you now."

Dawn moved closer to me, and we began to neck on the bench. I slid my hand under her t-shirt and raised it. While I fondled her breasts, she put her hand on my pants and was fondling me. We kept at it for an hour. She wasn't the girl I had known at school. I wondered how we would handle things in the fall.

After a while we stood and strolled hand in hand to an ice cream parlor. As we walked, she kept looking at me.

"Yes?"

"My, uh, parents are going out of town on Friday. They won't be back until Sunday morning. If you — if you want to come over, I can cook us dinner. You could spend the night."

"That sounds great. I have to work this weekend, but I can make it happen."

Over hot fudge sundaes, I told Dawn about my summer. I told her about Jack Flash, and about Uncle Don, Top Cat, and Get Lost Jimmy. We discussed my art. I couldn't believe I might be falling in love with this girl.

"I'll join you at the park on Friday," she said. "You can introduce me to Jack, and to the other people."

"That sounds great. Like I said, we're holding a small protest on Saturday for the homeless people who live in the park."

"Hell, yeah!" Dawn was enthusiastic. "I'll join you for that, too. I have friends who live in the park, actually. Well, friends might be too strong a word. I know people who live back in the wooded areas. I'll explain more Friday night."

"You know the bag ladies and the homeless men?"

"No. Not them. There are people our age who live there, too. You wouldn't know it unless you looked. They stay hidden for reasons." Dawn smiled at me.

"I saw some of them the other day. Bald heads or short haircuts, boots, suspenders, carrying weapons. The girls had their heads shaved, too. They looked like a rough bunch."

"That is a rough bunch. I don't have anything to do with that crowd. You've seen *The Warriors*. Remember The Turnbull ACs? That's what you were seeing. I'm talking about hanging out with the likes of The Orphans or maybe The Lizzies."

We finished our sundaes, and I walked Dawn home. On her corner I stopped and gave her another deep kiss. "I like you. A lot. I want to keep seeing you when school is going. So-help-me, if you turn back into the bitch you were — I'll pants you in front of the entire lunchroom."

"I won't. I want to hang with you, too. My so-called friends can go to Hell if they don't like it. I think it's time I started being who I am without hiding."

I laughed, "Who are you?"

"Friday night, Cyrus. You'll know Friday night."

I felt giddy and full of excess energy as I headed home. I watched the stars in the stars lighting up the sky and felt like bursting into song. My parents were already asleep when I arrived home. I wandered to my room, and a half hour later, with the help of a few articles in a magazine, the excess energy was dealt with. I lay on my bed thinking about Dawn until I drifted to sleep.

CHAPTER NINE

The next day I had time off from babysitting. Ms. Cramer said that Jack had a doctor appointment and that she needed to take him clothes shopping. I climbed out of bed and tossed my shorts into a hamper. Dawn had affected me more than I realized. After a long, cold shower, I got dressed and headed to the kitchen. Mrs. Ferrigno poured me a glass of orange juice, and as she put sausages and French toast on the griddle, I turned on the TV.

The guests on the talk show were children who had escaped abuse. I became engrossed in the tale of one girl who went on and on about her perfect life. Or, anyway, she claimed that others viewed it as perfect. Her parents were rich, and they provided material comforts galore. They rarely hit her, and they never touched her inappropriately. Her problem was that her parents ignored her. They were emotionally distant, and when they did pay attention, it was to hassle her about her grades, or about her lifestyle choices. They wanted her to fit into their social circles, and she felt that she couldn't. Once in a while they slapped her or took a strap to her if they became agitated with her behavior.

Most of the audience members didn't agree that this constituted abuse, and several claimed that she was ungrateful for all she had in life. The host quieted them down, and then brought on a professional to discuss the issues. The face of the professional was obscured because he said he was on an assignment for an article he was writing. He claimed to not want national publicity at the moment. The voice, however, sounded familiar. I couldn't place it, but I had heard it before.

Mrs. Ferrigno brought me breakfast and sat at the table to watch the show. The expert was explaining his views.

"Contrary to what some may believe, this young lady is experiencing a severe form of abuse. Constant emotional neglect can foster many future issues, especially when the abuse occurs in the early adolescent years. Emotional abuse is fully as traumatic and dangerous as physical abuse."

The phone rang, and I answered it. It was Dawn. "Cyrus, there's a talk show on channel twelve. You need to tune it in. I think you'll relate."

"I'm watching it. Hey, um, since you called, want to meet me at my fitness center at ten?"

"Sure. What's the address?"

I gave her the address and hung up. After helping with the dishes, I headed upstairs and changed into my gym shorts and a tank top. I put clean clothes in a knapsack for after my workout. Downstairs I secured my bike helmet, put my wallet and keys into a fanny-pack, grabbed my sack, and pulled off.

I enjoyed whizzing along with the wind to my back. The speed of my bike, and the freedom I felt while riding, was similar to the exhilaration that came over me when I was sketching nature or writing poetry. I stopped for a moment at the park to catch my breath. There were more homeless people walking along the paths than I had noticed over the past week.

I felt a swell of pride over my part in helping these people strike a blow for freedom. I felt empathy for these ragged men and women who were a microcosm of the macrocosm. My history teacher lectured often about our nation being founded on the principle that all men are created equal. That may have been true once upon a time, but it occurred to me that those with the means were a bit more equal than those without. Those who were born with less melanin were more equal than those who had active melanocytes. I felt this to be a universal truth.

I pulled off once more and rode to the fitness center. Arriving at the same time as Dawn, we locked our bikes together and I signed her in as my guest. She had a backpack of her own and was dressed in black spandex with pink racing stripes. It accentuated her positives. I let her proceed me down the hall. I mean with the outfit she was wearing – who wouldn't?

I secured my gear in a locker in the men's changing room and met Dawn in the lobby again. We headed to the room with the stationary bicycles, treadmills, and other equipment.

Dawn looked around. "What do you work out on?"

I pointed at the treadmills. "I usually start with five miles on that. Maximum speed and medium slope. If you aren't used to it, I suggest the stair climber or maybe a ski machine. You can also just set the treadmill to do a nice flat medium speed walk."

Dawn nodded and approached a treadmill next to me. I set my treadmill and began the warmup jog. In a few minutes I was sprinting at a forty-degree angle. The sweat was glistening, and my muscles were pulsating.

Dawn was going through her own workout and turned to look past me. I moved my head and saw that we had an audience. It wasn't the first time I had experienced that situation. There were regulars at the fitness center, many of them middle aged ladies. I worked out to kill time more than anything else, but those workouts had left me toned. When I looked in the mirror I could see the results, but I wasn't certain how I felt being ogled by ladies who were the age of my mother.

We finished our workout on the machines and moved to the weight room. I started by curling with the seventy-five-pound barbells. Dawn laid down on a bench and began to bench press. With each lift her breasts heaved. I lost count of my reps and finally stopped curling.

I loaded weights onto a bar, and Dawn spotted me while I did bench-presses. We did leg lifts and worked with a few nautilus machines until the sweat poured.

"So, what's next?" Dawn asked as she patted her face with a towel.

"I like to work out in the boxing room."

We entered a room that was full of tackling dummies, heavy bags, speed bags, and assorted gloves. I would never qualify for the sports teams in school, and I didn't much care to, but I worked out on the bags when I came to the gym. I found the action was a great way to clear my mind.

Dawn approached a heavy bag and held it, leaning over and bracing herself. I stepped up and began hitting it pretty hard without any protection. I hit it so hard, in fact, that Dawn was thrown clear and dumped on her backside. I laughed and so did she.

"I'll just sit against the wall and watch." Dawn stood and rubbed her butt.

I began working out on the speed bag. I began to feel my tensions ease. After I finished, I turned to look at Dawn and the tension returned. I still wasn't certain about her after the past year, but at that moment she was the most attractive girl I had ever known.

"To the hot tubs and steam sauna." I scooped her up and tossed her over my shoulder.

Dawn squealed, "Put me down! What are you doing?" She giggled.

I set her down outside the women's changing room and entered through the men's. We met on the other side by the pool and hot tub.

We had the steam room to ourselves, and after I stretched out on a bench, she sat between my legs and rested against me. We inhaled the steam as the nepenthe of the sauna cleansed us.

Dawn sighed, "that show this morning, it really spoke to me. I know that sounds crazy, but I understood where some of those people were coming from."

I stroked a hand gently over her chest. "It doesn't sound weird at all. I related to at least one of them, too. That girl whose parents ignore her unless they're irritated by something. Then they smack her around. She said that being rich didn't mean that much to her. She wanted to do more to help others."

"Yeah. I totally got that. It's hard to say this, but I need to. I wish I could find the words."

"Just talk. The words will come."

"I'm not who I pretend to be in school. I know what you and others see; a snobby princess who hangs out with other rich bitches and judges everyone. The thing is, I could be spending my summer at the country club. I don't want to. I told you that no one else is around, but that's not entirely true."

I shifted a bit and held Dawn closer. "Yeah? Really? And, yes, that is what I think about you and your clique. You asked me to get together though, and honestly, you're physically attractive. I figured why not settle for what I could get? Also, I meant it about what I'd do if you start that stuff again when school starts up."

"I know, and I'd deserve it and worse. Like I was saying, Christina, Hope, Faith, Trish, Venus, Heather, they're who my parents expect me to hang out with. Especially my mother. Christina and Faith are both home this summer, but they spend every day at the country club hanging out with and the cool guys and jocks. I don't want to do that anymore."

"Why is that? Why the sudden change?"

"It isn't sudden. I've wanted to escape all of that for a while. I do sometimes, too. I just have to keep it under wraps."

"I see." I ran a hand over her flat belly and kissed her lightly on the cheek. "I'm sorry if I misjudged you."

"You didn't. I told you, whatever comes my way I deserve it for how I acted. I just...I can't explain it well. My mother is pretty famous for her books and radio talk show. My stepfather is a CFO and works his butt off. They both drink a lot, but I guess that comes with being yuppie class. They don't abuse me, really, but they don't show me much affection. They buy their love from me like they buy everything else. The only time things get bad is if they think I'm bringing negative attention their way. If I do anything that makes people look at them as less than perfect, I pay for it."

We sat a while longer just inhaling the steam. Holding Dawn between my legs I felt my spirit revive and soar. Despite the difficulties of our respective lives, there was a primal energy that emanated from each of us; that fed into the other. I had never felt anything similar in my fifteen years of life.

We stood and stepped out into the cooler air surrounding the pool and hot tub. I took Dawn's hand and helped her into the hot whirlpool water. The hot tub felt sensational after our work out.

"I understand most of what you're saying. My life is pretty much the same way. I think my parents don't know how to tell me that they care. In fact, I don't know that they do, in fact, care. My mother says that they didn't plan to have me. I was an inconvenience in their relationship, but that they do their best to love me anyway. She regards me as ungrateful because I don't want to be an assistant at a bank or a law firm every summer."

Dawn and I held hands under water. "I have some friends who aren't in school. People I know. I can only see them if I sneak out or tell my parents I'm staying with another friend and then escape for the night. Those girls at school are my cover. I hang out with them, and then no one suspects that I'm not who they think."

"I asked you before who you really are. You plan to tell me?"

"On Friday, Cyrus. I guess what I'm asking is can you forgive me. I'd do anything to get you to forgive me. And I mean anything. I looked at you all year, and I thought about you a lot. I had no way to tell you how I felt because you hang out with the fa...um the art crowd and the..."

"The what? Losers? They may be losers, but they aren't fake. I understand why you act the way you do, but don't ever call art students what you were about to call us. I'm as straight as they come. Most of the kids in the art classes are."

"I corrected myself. I'm sorry. It's like I live two different lives and they cross into each other."

"So, these friends of yours in the park...they definitely aren't those hard looking dudes and chicks I saw the other day, right? I have to admit that although I put on a brave front for Jack, I was sort of scared of them."

"Hell, no! I want nothing to do with the baldies. You better stay away from them, too. You should be scared. That's not me being judgmental, either. Those shaved skull cretins are bad news. I mean bad as in they'll kill you because you look at them wrong. No, Cyrus, my friends aren't like that. They're punk rockers, and they're homeless, but they aren't psychopaths."

"Good to know. I enjoy punk bands, but I haven't had a lot of opportunity to explore the scene. I don't want to come across as some elitist. That's my parents. I just don't want a mudhole stomped in my ass, you know?"

"I completely get that. Just stay away from the baldies and you'll be fine. Everyone else is pretty much live and let live."

We sat in silence for a while in the swirling water. Dawn leaned against me and began rubbing me under the water. I began rubbing her as well. Soon we were making out and moaning. I stopped for a breath, looked up, and saw that we had been in the hot tub a while. We looked like raisins.

A half hour later, Dawn emerged from the changing room dressed in shorts and an Eight Ball T-shirt. I raised my eyebrows. "I didn't know you liked Eight Ball. I took you for a Bangals or Tiffany fan."

"You'd be surprised. Desperate Ones, Fugazi, Government Issue, I like that kind of music. I just can't listen to it at home much."

I smiled. "Guess you never can tell just by looking. Hey, want some lunch? I'm buying."

CHAPTER TEN

I t was one in the afternoon when we entered the coffee shop across the street from the fitness center. Dawn ordered a grilled smoked gouda with sun-dried tomato and avocado, and a double shot cappuccino. I said to make mine the same.

As we ate, I told Dawn more about how my summer had been. We talked about literature, and art. Dawn was well read, better than I was in fact. I made a few notes of some authors she suggested like Hunter S. Thompson and Lawrence Ferlinghetti. They sounded like they were up there with Leary, Kerouac, and Burroughs.

"I don't much feel like going home right now, and I don't have to work today. Want to go to a movie? The mall?" I left a five-dollar tip.

"The mall sounds good. I just hope we don't see anyone from school there." Dawn stood.

"If we do, we do. You need to stop hiding whoever it is that you are. I don't let my parents dictate who I am, you shouldn't let yours dictate who you are."

"I guess. There's more to it. You'll find out..."

"Friday, I know." I interrupted her and she stuck out her tongue at me.

We biked to the mall and locked our rides to a rack. As we walked through the mall, hand in hand, I spotted a jewelry store. There were benefits to being upper-middle class, and I thought about something Dawn had said to me.

"Let's go in there," I pointed to the store. "I want to look at something."

"What's in there that we can afford?" Dawn followed me.

"Don't ask questions. You said earlier that you'd do anything if I forgave you. That puts me in charge. I began perusing the items on the lower end of the price scale.

The salesman approached me. "Can I help you find something?"

"I was wondering the price on that white gold ring with the small diamond chip. And the necklace?"

The man brightened. "Yes, sir. Those are nice items. The ring would be $193.00 and the necklace $77.00 I can even size the ring for no additional charge."

Dawn looked at me as her mouth opened and realization filled her eyes. "Cyrus, you don't..."

I glared at her, "Quiet, you. You said something earlier. I'm holding you to it."

The salesman took the measure of Dawn's left ring finger, and then matched the ring to it from a set he had in the back. I paid him for the items, and we left the store. I led Dawn to an area in the center of the mall that had oversized chairs and a few couches for people to rest between excursions into stores.

"Dawn, you said that you would do anything to be forgiven. You know this."

"I know what I said. What's this all about?" She laughed nervously.

"I forgive you for being how you were this past year. But now you have to wear this ring and necklace. It's a promise ring. You wear these and then you don't forget whose you are."

"Whose I am? Excuse me? You don't own me, Cyrus. I'm sorry for how I acted, but I'm not property."

I shook my head. "I didn't mean it like that. I want you to be my girl. In school, out of school, always. I'll watch out for you and so help me if anyone starts anything with you in school."

"You do understand. I can't be your girl, though."

"I get it. Your parents expect..."

Dawn giggled and then kissed me. "Would you settle for us being each other's? That's what I meant."

I placed the ring on her finger and attached the clasp behind the necklace. "I think that's the best offer I've ever had."

Dawn and I sat on a couch as she eyed the ring and snuggled into me. We stood and kept walking. Dawn checked the ring several times as if she couldn't believe I had bought it for her. She fingered the necklace as well, and a few times I caught her looking in mirrors at stores and smiling.

We stopped in a ladies' boutique, and Dawn bought a few blouses. She pulled me into a Victoria's Secret, and I couldn't help but blush.

"Um, this isn't a store for guys." I started to back out the door.

"Oh, come on. I need advice. Don't you think this would look super darling on me?" She held up a pink teddy. "Or this?" She held up a black lace thong and bra set.

"I admit that the idea of seeing you in those interests me, but I have no idea how to advise you on that? I don't know what is or isn't good quality for the money."

Dawn laughed. "It isn't about quality. It's about whether... like you said it sparks your interest. I'll buy a few things. Hey, they have this in leopard print, too."

After our shopping, we stopped at the food court and bought sodas. We sat and Dawn yawned. "I haven't run around this much in weeks. So, you were telling me about this kid you babysit for. That there's some kind of protest in the park Saturday?"

"Yeah. The people who live there, the homeless people, they used to be able to get bratwurst at the hotdog carts. Now they can't because it isn't cost effective to sell those versus hotdogs which can be bought cheaper and sold at a greater profit."

"Well, I think it's very civic minded of you to help them." Dawn sipped her coke with a pinky extended. I laughed.

"The kid I babysit for is named Jeremiah Carlson Cramer, but he calls himself Jack Flash."

"Cute. Like the kid's cartoon.? I take it he isn't a Stones fan. He a good kid?"

"He's pretty cool. He's smart, and he asks a lot of good questions. I get the feeling that he's upset about things at times, but I can't put my finger on what's the matter. His mother is one of those health food nuts, and she is beyond stuffy. I picture her being like you in high school – well the old you."

"Ugh. Well, I can't wait to meet him. He sounds precious."

We chatted a while and then decided to catch a matinee. The movie was one of the standard summer comedies that are full of innuendo, and cheap jokes about current events. Dawn snuggled against me as much as the seats would allow, and we held hands. I tried to remember how I felt even a few days before. I was happier than I had been in a long while.

After the movie we biked to our respective houses. I began to mentally prepare for the events of the next two days. My nerves were overactive, and I felt like jumping around. I knew that it was as much about Dawn as it was about anything else. I had to restrain myself from calling her on the phone the minute I got in the door.

My parents had a cocktail party to attend, and Mrs. Ferrigno had the night off. I defrosted a steak and changed into my sweats while it was cooking. I fried three eggs and some hashbrowns. Once my dinner was prepared, I took the plate to my room and put on my earphones to listen to a tape of Minor Threat. After dinner, I put the dishes in the dishwasher, and headed to bed. I had to babysit early, and Dawn was meeting me and Jack at the park.

CHAPTER ELEVEN

I woke to some radio announcer telling me that I needed to try a new hair replacement system. I pushed a button to silence the noise. Sliding out of bed, I did some calisthenics and stretches, and took a shower. After dressing I headed downstairs.

Mrs. Ferrigno was watching one of the morning talk shows. She brought me a plate of sausages and grits with half a cantaloupe and cottage cheese. I poured myself a glass of juice.

During a commercial I looked up. "Hey, Mrs. F, did you ever protest anything?"

She looked over at me from where she was doing the dishes. "Sure, I did. I protested for women's rights, an end to nuclear arms, an end to apartheid, lots of issues when I was younger."

"Yeah, but what if someone wanted something, I mean really wanted it, but it lacked that level of gravitas. Like say they wanted something to be sold somewhere, and the proprietors didn't listen for economic reasons?"

"Listen to me, Francis. If a person wants something, and if no one will listen to them, then a protest is a good way to make them open their ears." Mrs. Ferrigno placed the frying pans in the drainer rack.

"I agree with you." I finished my breakfast and rinsed my

dishes before turning on the dishwasher. "I'm off to work, Mrs. F. I'll see you for dinner."

I arrived at the Cramer household, and Jack was excited to see me. He already had his sweater on and was squirming on the couch. Ms. Cramer said that she wanted to speak with me, and we stepped into her kitchen.

"Cyrus, I wanted to inform you that I am pleased with the job you are doing. Jeremiah has taken a liking to you, and you appear to be capable of caring for his needs. However, I have noticed that he has been engaging in entirely too much fantasy play."

"Fantasy play? He hasn't shown any signs of that while we walk in the park. I'm not certain I understand."

Last night he was in his room pretending to play a guitar. He was talking to people who weren't there. He called one of them Uncle Don and another he called Jimmy. If you notice anything, please let me know. I can have him examined by a child psychiatrist."

I spoke in hushed tones, "I'll keep an eye on him. If I notice anything out of the ordinary, I'll let you know."

"I appreciate that." Ms. Cramer led the way back to the living room. I stood by the door, and Jack joined me.

Two blocks later I knelt to help Jack remove his sweater. "We need to chat, buddy. You aren't in trouble, but we need to get something clear."

Jack looked at me and started to cry. "Did I do something bad? Are you going to stop playing with me? I'm sorry, Cyrus."

I gave him a comforting hug and dried his tears. "No, buddy. You didn't do anything bad. It's just that you can't even talk about what we do when you're home. You can't pretend to be Top Cat anymore. You can't talk about Uncle Don or Get Lost

Jimmy or Hetty. You're mother doesn't understand what we do, and she'll fire me. Then for sure we can't hang out anymore."

Jack nodded and hugged me. "She's one of the bad guys. She said my friends were imaginary. I told her that they were not and that she was imaginary. She smacked me and put me in the corner. When she wasn't looking, I zapped her with my lasers."

"I understand, buddy. Please don't say anything about our adventures, OK? Just read your books and watch TV. You can't tell her what we do, or she'll make you be Jeremiah all the time."

I laughed at the thought of a five-year-old jumping around playing air guitar. We arrived at a corner deli across from the park and standing there with a paper bag in her hand was Dawn. She extracted five Jack Flash comic books and handed them to Jack.

I scooped up Jack. "Jack Flash this is Dawn Larkspur. Dawn, this is Jack."

Dawn smiled at Jack. "Hey, little man. What's happening?"

Jack scowled, "My name is Jack! I'm not little. I'm just fine, thank you." He gave her a Bronx cheer which she returned.

"Cyrus told me a lot about you, Jack. That's why I bought you those comics to read."

Jack looked Dawn up and down. "Girls are yucky. They have girl germs." Jack said.

"Hey, Jack, wanna come over some time and make mud pies? Or maybe we can climb trees." Dawn entered the deli, and we followed.

Jack looked suspicious. "Girls don't do that stuff. They play house, and dolls, and pull my hair at school."

Dawn laughed, "I think they just like you."

Jack shook his head, "They aren't being very nice if they like me. I don't pull their hair."

I set Jack down and we ordered donuts and coffee. I ordered hot milk with a shot of coffee for Jack. After we ate, we walked across the street to the park and Jack ran to the swings. I sat on the teeter-totter with Dawn and watched Jack swing.

We were enjoying the morning when the sound of music came across the breeze. Jack jumped off the swing and screamed "Top Cat!" He was off like a shot. Dawn and I followed him. We approached a bench and there was Top Cat and Get Lost Jimmy playing. They greeted us and kept going.

Top Cat played several songs about Minneapolis, Minnesota. He mentioned between sets that he had lived there for a while. Uncle Don arrived later than usual, and he had with him a picnic basket.

"Good afternoon my friends. I was hoping you might be here." He spread out a tablecloth and unloaded sandwiches, chips, and sodas.

"Uncle Don, Top Cat, Jimmy, this is my girlfriend, Dawn." I said.

Dawn did a polite curtsey. "I've heard a lot about all of you from Cyrus. I'm planning to attend the protest tomorrow."

Uncle Don looked at the group. "I'll be here, but afterward I might be absent for a week or so. I heard from my job, and matters are moving along. Management is willing to negotiate, and I must be there. I'll return after that business is complete, if only to lock up my summer home."

A few hours, and a stroll around the gardens later, Dawn and I took Jack home. Dawn stayed out of sight as I walked Jack to his door. I assured Ms. Cramer that I had noted nothing unusual in his behavior. She told me that was a relief and asked if I was available for future overnight babysitting.

I stepped off the porch and met Dawn halfway down the block.

We walked to my house, and I introduced her to Mrs. Ferrigno. Dawn and I grabbed a couple cans of Coke and headed up to my room where I began packing items for the night.

Dawn sat on my bed perusing my collection of magazines. "You're truly debased, Cyrus. I mean these girls are so obviously airbrushed, and they must have had enhancements to get their breasts that perfect. What the heck is this?" She held up a copy of *Bondage Beauties.*

"You interested in that stuff?" I smiled at her and raised my eyebrows.

Dawn shrugged, "Uh, well...not this exactly." She blushed.

I secured the straps and grabbed my sack. We headed downstairs and left. I had informed my parents that I was spending the night at a friend's house, and they had said that was fine. They were in the middle of an argument and had no time to say anything hurtful to me, being too busy saying such things to each other.

Dawn and I passed a drugstore several blocks away and she pulled me inside. "Cyrus, we need to get something here." I stammered and blushed when she handed me a box of King George Lambskin Prophylactics.

We walked to the counter. "I'd like to purchase these." I tried to look natural.

The clerk didn't bat an eye as she rang me up. I paid and Dawn and I exited. My spirits began to soar as I placed the bag in my knapsack. I was walking hand in hand with the most beautiful girl in school, and apparently, I was going to be having actual intercourse for the first time. I kept looking at Dawn and then looking away.

"Yes? Something wrong?" Dawn blushed a little herself.

"Nothing. I just...I never would have suspected..."

"What? That I'm sexually active? There's a lot you don't know, Cyrus. Also, I'd appreciate it if you kept everything tonight to yourself. I have a reputation to protect. You know?"

"I wasn't planning on telling every guy in school that I planted my flag on one of the cool bitches. You still planning on changing how you treat me and my friends?"

"Of course I am. I just...it's OK. I'm sorry. Yes, I'm changing how I treat people, I'm learning to be me instead of who everyone thinks I should be."

We arrived at her house, and she told me to let her make like a hostess. She grabbed my sack and headed to her room. I began watching the news and must have dozed off. Dawn shook me awake and in front of us were two standing trays with plates of grilled flounder, peas, asparagus, and bread. She had poured glasses of Montrachet.

"Have mercy. Where did you learn to cook like this? And where did you get the wine? My parents would kick my ass until Hell wouldn't have it if I touched their supply." I took a bite of fish.

"This isn't my parents. You hide magazines, I hide other things. Like this wine. I took some cooking classes last summer at the country club." Dawn turned off the TV and pushed a different remote. A CD started, and El Grande filled the room singing "Anti-Reincarnation Chant." We listened to the entire CD as we ate.

"I seriously never took you for a fan of this kind of music. I love how he mixes folk music, Indian chanting, Native American style rhythms, African war chants, and punk overtones."

He's a musical genius. So are Eight Ball. That's probably one of my favorite punk bands other than The Ramones and Virgin Prunes." Dawn started clearing dishes and I helped.

After we finished drying the dishes, we walked to Dawn's bedroom, and she put on a tape of Eight Ball. As we were listening, Dawn reached under her bed. My eyes widened as she retrieved a bong, and a bag of marijuana buds.

"Damn! How long have you been using drugs? You really aren't who I thought you were!"

"I've been smoking out for about six months. Mom's a pain in the ass, and Dad isn't any better. I have to escape their constant screaming at me and the pressure they put on me. I also need to escape those idiots I hang out with at school."

"Idiots? Since when?"

Dawn shook her head. "You can't forgive me, can you? I said I'm sorry."

I smiled at her. "I forgive you. I'm just in shock at the sudden change."

Dawn loaded the bong and demonstrated the use of it. I took my first hit, and nothing happened. I took two more tokes, and suddenly something did happen. I felt myself thrown backwards internally. My peripheral vision went away, and my mind took me through a lucid dreamlike state. Everything slowed down like I was enveloped in a thick fog.

Dawn turned on two black light lamps and a strobe light, and I began dancing to the music. Dawn joined me and we held each other as we vibrated in unison through the strobe effects.

When the tape ended, I began tickling her. She laughed and squirmed, and we moved toward her bed. I knew instinctively that I was ready, and began raising her t-shirt, she helped me remove it and then she removed mine. We continued like that, the final act being me putting on my protection. We had both heard enough in health class about the possibilities if I didn't.

The next half hour was as enjoyable as anything I had ever

experienced, and after a rest, and another smoke, we continued. Around eleven at night, and three condoms later, I carried her naked into the bathroom and placed her in the tub. We ran warm water and added some Black Orchid bubble bath. She had moved her boombox to the bathroom door, and "Miles in The Sky" by Miles Davis played as we soaked.

After a while we climbed out and dried each other. We smoked a few more hits and walked downstairs to watch a movie. Dawn put in "Heathers." After the first movie, Dawn put in a DVD of "The Breakfast Club." By the time the second movie was over we were yawning. We fell asleep on the floor wrapped in each other's arms.

CHAPTER TWELVE

We woke at seven and made our way upstairs. I had a residual headache, and my stomach felt a bit sour. Dawn took a shower while I got my gear together. While I waited for her, I looked through some of her books. She had quite a collection of philosophy books as well as a few by Carlos Castaneda and some Judy Blume novels. Behind the books I spotted some DVDs she had hidden. I was looking through them when Dawn walked in.

"You found my secret stash, huh?"

"I noticed they were behind the books and thought I'd take a peek."

"I like those three by Umbra Road. The two that say Road Trip on them aren't bad, either. They're about students from an all-girls boarding school who are rewarded with a road trip for being good students, but they do run into trouble with the chaperones."

"I read the back blurbs. You like that sort of thing?"

"Asks the guy with the stash of porno magazines." Dawn smiled at me.

"I'm not knocking it. I was curious. Maybe we could watch one of these some time."

"We could. You might get some ideas about how to forgive

me for the way I acted last year."

"You certainly keep the real you well hidden. I would have never suspected that you were into drugs, sex, and like that."

"That's the general idea. I doubt my parents suspect anything, and that's the way I want it."

"We have to pick up Jack Flash soon. We can grab coffee on the way to the park, and around noon is the protest."

Dawn nodded. "Go have your shower."

As we walked toward Jack's a half hour later, Dawn looked over at me. "You nervous about this?"

"Maybe a little. I hope the police don't show up. I've never done anything like this, but I've read about these things going south in a hurry."

"It'll be OK. Anyway, we're going to be on the sidelines with the kid."

"That's true." I finished my espresso and chased the last crumbs of pastry on my plate.

We proceeded to Jack's neighborhood, and Dawn stopped down the block to sit on a wall surrounding a yard. I walked to the door and knocked.

"Hello, Cyrus." Ms. Cramer looked me up and down. "Is there some reason you're dressed in that manner? You look like one of the poor children from the other side of the tracks."

"My apologies. This was all that I had to wear that was clean. The washer is being repaired. I'll wash my clothes tonight."

Ms. Cramer nodded at me. Jack appeared from upstairs, looking subdued and dressed in his sweater and jeans. He and I bid Ms. Cramer farewell and walked down the block. Dawn stood and joined us. Two blocks later Jack removed his sweater and I put it in my backpack.

"I get to sing today, right? At the protest?" Jack smiled up at me.

"You sure do, buddy. Is anything wrong? You looked sad coming down the stairs."

"I'm fine. Mommy gets mad about stuff and sometimes I'm really trying to be good. She yelled at me because I asked her who this man was that she was talking to last night. He doesn't speak English very well. I didn't mean to be rude, but she told me to go to my room and stay there. Later she came up and smacked me and yelled at me for interrupting adults." Jack looked at me and Dawn. "You guys are lucky. You don't have adults telling you what to do."

Dawn scooped Jack up and carried him. "Don't bet on it, buddy. I get yelled at plenty. I still get smacked sometimes, too. Today, though, we're going to make something right for people. We're going to make adults listen."

"We have to stay to the side. Top Cat and Uncle Don said so. We did help, though. We made the signs and I'm going to sing." Jack pointed at the park.

I didn't know how he managed it, but Top Cat had a crowd gathered. The crowd was a bizarre conglomeration of muttering, shuffling old men and women. They were attired in ragged coats, baggy sweaters, faded suits, torn sports jackets, sneakers and sandals, rubber boots and hiking boots, pantyhose, dress socks, baseball caps and formal hats. They carried purses, garbage bags, backpacks, and briefcases. Several pushed carts with their belongings in them.

Top Cat approached and reminded us to stay put on the sidelines. If any trouble started, we were to walk away from the area and stay away. Uncle Don concurred with these orders. Get Lost Jimmy sat with us, his dog Swee'Pea at his feet.

Jack looked up, "I still get to sing, right?"

Top Cat gave him a thumbs up. "Of course, dude. You also have to hand out the signs."

Jack picked up the signs four at a time and handed them to the ragtag bunch of marchers. The signs read "Bring Back the Bratwurst!" with a picture of a hotdog surrounded by a red circle with a line through it.

I looked over at Top Cat. "Do you ever play anything like "We're Not Gonna Take It" by Twisted Sister? Or any punk rock tunes?"

Top Cat chuckled, "I do at times. I also know what draws a crowd in this park and what makes money."

After the last sign was handed out, and Jack was sitting between me and Dawn, the protestors lined up. When Top Cat shouted charge, they marched forward. Good Lord did they march. They had already attracted a crowd, and as the moved forward muttering to themselves, they attracted even more people.

The hotdog vendor looked worried, and then, to the amusement of the crowd, Top Cat began to play his guitar and Jimmy joined in on harmonica. Jack began singing the chorus of Blowing in The Wind. The vendor was at first amused, and then became agitated. After a group of men in business suits joined the marchers, the vendor became irate.

"Bring back the bratwurst!" The men in suits began to chant. The group of homeless people took up the cry.

I prepared to leave with Jack and Dawn when a police officer approached and asked Top Cat what was the problem. The officer nodded as Top Cat spoke. Then the cop smiled and approached the vendor and spoke to him.

The cop turned and faced the crowd. "What is it that you want from this?" His voice boomed and the crowd went silent.

"We want bratwurst to be once again sold in this park." Top Cat replied.

"So," The officer smiled, "if I secure a promise that bratwurst will be sold then you'll disperse?"

"If the promise is in good faith." Top Cat nodded. "We have nowhere else to be and all day to get there."

The vendor threw up his hands, "OK. Alright. I sell bratwurst again. You just had better buy them. They cost more and if you don't buy, I have to stop selling them."

"Now we're talking! We just won! Everyone split." Top Cat shouted to the crowd. They dropped their signs and walked away.

Dawn, Jack, and I collected the signs and various other items that had been left behind. We lay the signs on the bench and looked back at the cop.

He had a broad smile for us. "This beat is better already. Nice to know someone cares besides me."

I stared at the cop my eyes wide and my mouth open. I was pleased that he agreed with our cause, and yet I couldn't believe that a cop could be that reasonable. I also felt a peculiar stirring inside my chest. We had struck a blow for freedom and had succeeded. Yes, it was something ludicrous like the freedom to have a bratwurst, but denial of freedom anywhere was a threat to freedom everywhere.

My mind began racing as I looked for my next cause. The feeling of victory was addictive. I needed something with more gravitas, something significant for which to fight. I had no clue what that something was, but I was determined to find it.

Jack interrupted my reverie. He was pulling on my arms and jumping around. "We won! We did it! We're the heroes!"

"Easy, tiger. Chill please. You and Cyrus stay here, I'll be back." Dawn ruffled Jack's hair.

I looked around, and everyone had dispersed. I took Jack to the swings and noticed that Dawn was approaching a wooded section further along. An older teen with long black hair, dressed in jeans and a leather vest over his bare chest, stepped out of the woods. He appeared to know Dawn. She reached into her pocket, and then shook hands with the man. She returned to me and Jack and sat on a swing.

"You really do hang out with the crowd who live over there?" I asked.

"I told you I know some of them. I do business on occasion. They're not bad people, you know?"

"I don't know, no. My understanding is that the homeless teens in this park carry guns and knives. They use hard drugs and have lengthy criminal records. I admit that's their business, but I have Jack with me now."

Dawn laughed, "now who's acting like a rich snob?" She shook her head. "You shouldn't judge people based on your lifestyle or mine. The kids who hang out and live around here aren't bad. They're misunderstood, and they're harassed by the police and others. They have to protect themselves, and sometimes that means using violence."

I looked Dawn up and down. "You really are nothing like the act you put on in school."

"You don't even know that half of it, Cyrus. I wish I could live out here. I feel more alive out here. These kids are my friends – well, in a way they are. You and I are lucky. Jack is, too. We have nice homes and good food to eat. Our parents may be pains in the butt, but at least we have parents. Those kids you're looking down on have no homes, no love, nada, and zip. They were either kicked out, abandoned, or had to run from serious abuse. They've had it hammered into them every day of their life that anyone can do anything to them and escape consequences for doing it. The authorities don't care. Most of them have suffered every imaginable evil. They've been forced to march in lock step to whatever point they are told. Everything they ever received was rationed out. They learned that the only recourse is to hide; to avoid all people who aren't like them. Teachers, parents, all adults they ever encountered made up lies about them. They put those on their official records, and then those records are looked at any time the authorities want to hassle them. They're branded guilty before they even get a trial."

I stood and pulled Dawn to me. We hugged and I rubbed her behind softly. 'I didn't know that. I'm sorry for what I said. I've never actually met any of them. I just figured they wanted to be left alone."

Jack came over and hugged us both. "I'm hungry. Can we get a snack?"

I looked at my watch and realized that it was time to take him home. We stopped at a corner store and purchased candy bars and Cokes. Jack gobbled his candy bar like he hadn't eaten all day. As we approached his house, Dawn sat on a stone wall in front of a house, and I wiped the chocolate from Jack's mouth.

Ms. Cramer met us at the door and looked worried. My stomach fell and I began to think up excuses for why we were late getting Jack home. Ms. Cramer shooed Jack inside.

"Go upstairs and look at a book or play quietly, Jeremiah. I need to speak to Cyrus." She turned toward me. "I need to ask you a favor, and it is a bit of an imposition."

I nodded. "Ask away, ma'am."

"I have to attend some meetings out of the country. I was only informed about them three hours ago. I have to go to Mexico and to Colombia in ten days. I'll be gone for five days. I was hoping that you could watch Jeremiah for that length of time. I understand that you most likely have other activities in your life. As I said, it's an imposition, but if you say no, I have no idea whom to ask."

"I would be pleased to do that. You understand, of course, that I need to ask permission. I'll let you know in less than three hours. When would you need me to be here?"

"Early in the morning a week from Tuesday. I will return the following Saturday in the early evening. If you can do this, I will pay you five-hundred dollars plus expenses if there are any."

"I'll head home and ask my parents, ma'am." We shook hands.

I returned to where Dawn was sitting, and she hopped down from the wall. "I thought you'd abandoned me. Took you long enough." She giggled.

"Ms. Cramer needed to discuss business. If I can get permission, I might be babysitting for five days straight a week from Tuesday. I'll make enough to cover art supplies for the entire school year."

"That's awesome. Hey, if you like we can hook up and I'll help babysit. I don't need money, just time with you. I'd just have to tell my parents that I'm staying at Hope Bradley's house. Her sister and her will cover for me if my parents call."

"Sounds like a plan. I know Jack likes having you around."

Dawn smiled at me, and we kissed. She reached into her pocket and pulled out two plastic bags. One of them was clearly marijuana. The other was a brownish substance I didn't recognize. She'd made a buy in the park, and I hadn't even noticed.

"What is that?"

"This is the answer to every artist's needs. Pot, and shrooms. I figured that some night when you don't have to work the next day, we could drop mushrooms. Maybe in the park. Maybe we could hang out at my house again and you could draw me."

"I could try. I don't have a great deal of experience drawing models, yet."

I walked Dawn home and headed to my house. My parents were both home, and that meant that I would need to shower and clean up before dinner.

CHAPTER THIRTEEN

D inner with my parents was not on my list of favorite activities. For one thing, my parents expected me to dress in what they considered appropriate attire. That meant polo shirts, slacks, or chinos, and with my hair combed. I saw no reason to go to the trouble of looking like a yuppie youth unless company was coming. In fact, I saw no fit reason to dress up in that situation, either.

All the primping and posturing was due to the fact that my mother felt it reflected poorly on our family if I was seen to dress like a normal teen. Unless I was working out in the gym, wearing a t-shirt and shorts was considered the look of poor white trash. My father was of the belief that if I dressed in semi-formal attire, it would change my mindset. He was certain that if I dressed like an office clerk, I would gain an interest in attending law school.

I looked at myself in the mirror, and for the hundredth time wished that I had the nerve to tell my parents where to shove their pretensions. I had no interest in studying the law or ever becoming a lawyer. I did read about certain crimes, and criminals, but that was for other reasons. I was interested in people my age who had either blown a fuse or who had stuck it to the system. Most of the time I felt close to blowing my circuits, but something kept me from doing so. I had fantasies about blowing away some of the jerks in my school...and my parents. I knew I would never actually do so, and I didn't know why some people finally did snap like that. There was no one I could reasonably ask about it, so instead I studied the subject myself. I got what my English teacher called a vicarious sense of satisfaction.

I entered the dining room and took my seat. "Hello, Mother. Hello, Father. How are you this evening?"

My mother gave me a look. "I've had a trying day. Don't start any trouble."

"I'm doing well, son," my father served himself from a platter of fish. "I spoke with Henry Mulligan at my firm. I believe I can set you up with an internship as an office boy next summer."

I nodded and served myself. My father assumed that he was doing me a grand favor, and I didn't care to disabuse him of that notion. Any strenuous objections would lead to an argument, and my mother was already in a testy mood.

My mother looked up from her food. "An office boy in a law firm? Him? I'd like to see that, but he's a lost cause. Francis can hardly be bothered to dress properly unless he's forced. Honestly, Francis, I think that you dress and act as you do to embarrass your father and me. I mean just the other day I was at the beauty salon, and I heard Agatha Yahr talking about her son winning a golf scholarship to a university. He may be working as a caddy, but he's networking with corporate CEO's and CFO's. Her daughter, Trisch, is a clerk at a major modeling firm. Agatha asked me what you're doing this summer. I was ashamed to tell her that you're a babysitter."

I cleared my throat, "yes, Mother. I'll give thought to the

law offer for next summer. In the meantime, I do need to ask permission for something."

My father looked over at me. "Yes, son?"

"Ms. Cramer has an urgent meeting that suddenly came up. It is out of the country, and she needs me to babysit for several days in succession. A week from Tuesday. I informed her that I could not make that decision without first asking your permission."

My mother scowled at me. "I suppose we must allow you to do this. I'm still surprised that a socialite like her would allow a lazy child like you to care for her own child. However, if we don't allow this then you'll be coming to us for money."

My father sighed, "Enough, dear. I appreciate that you have the foresight to ask first instead of simply accepting such a request. I admit that it is embarrassing to have you babysitting while the children of my colleagues are making future contacts that will pay high dividends. However, if you have to babysit you at least chose the right caliber of clientele."

I took a bite and chewed. "I might one day want to be the legal advocate for children in court. This job gives me some knowledge about the subjects with whom I'd be dealing."

My parents looked at me, stunned into silence. My father recovered quickly. "The Cramer boy is hardly the type of child with whom you'd be working, but you make a compelling case for yourself."

My mother watched as Mrs. Ferrigno served our dessert. Once the Raspberry sherbet and chocolate cake was served, we resumed our conversation. My mother gave me a sharp look. "I am shocked that you have any future plans at all. Do realize that if you are going to take this assignment, you had better not call on us when you run into trouble. You're old enough to do this then you're old enough to handle any problems on your own."

I was free. For the job at least. My feelings about what she had said rankled, but they often did. I would have thought that by then I wouldn't care what she thought about me, but I had to admit that her words hurt. I sat in silence eating my dessert while she and my father had their own discussion and ignored me once more.

After excusing myself and putting my dishes in the dishwasher, I returned upstairs. I put a CD of The Talking Heads into my stereo, adjusted my earphones, and began writing a poem.

Childish Dreams
and libidinous thoughts
of the callipygian other sex.
Mother Nature's stroking force
shoots the moon
as the cadenza blows.
And the candy man roasts
On a manual spit.

I felt pleased with the poem, albeit the subject matter was obvious. I decided to take it to art class with me and show it to Mr. K.

"Hot Damn! I did it. I got through to one of my students!" Mr. K. beamed at me after reading my poem. "Cyrus, you're really letting loose with your soul. This is amazing!"

I shrugged. "It's OK. I was thinking about this girl I'm getting to know. She's different. She makes me feel different. It's not easy to say what's inside."

"This poem says it all, Cyrus. Says it all."

After class I returned home and tried to listen to music or

read my magazines. I couldn't focus. I had too much Dawn on my mind. I rose and had a good stretch. It was half past nine, but I needed to take a walk.

I went downstairs and stopped in the kitchen where Mrs. Ferrigno was eating some pie and watching a romance movie. "Hey. I'm going for a walk. I'll be back whenever. No need to wait up for me."

She looked over at me and then back to the television. "That's good. Your parents went out with some people from your father's office."

I walked to Dawn's house and looked up at the windows on the second floor. Hers was lit up. I thought about tossing a pebble at it like people do in the movies, but I always suspected that a window would break doing that. I was trying to think of a way to get her attention when she walked to the window and looked out. I waved at her.

Dawn was downstairs and out the door in under five minutes. She had on tight jeans, an Operation Ivy t-shirt, and pink converse high-tops. She stepped off the porch and smiled at me. "What are you doing standing down here?"

"I didn't want to ring the bell this late and tossing rocks at your window seemed like a dangerous proposition."

"You could have called me. I have my own phone in my room." Dawn gave me a kiss.

"Yeah. I came home from class tonight, and I couldn't think about anything but you. You fill my thoughts all day and night anymore?" I wished I hadn't said it as the words came out of my mouth. It sounded so corny.

Dawn hugged me, her chest pressing into mine. "I think about you, too, Cyrus. You're different than any guy I ever knew. You're not like my parents, or like the cool guys at school.

You come across much closer to the teens on the park than you do to the snobs who live around here." She motioned to her neighborhood.

"Snobs?" I was incredulous. "Who are you to call anyone a snob?"

"That isn't a fair shot, and you know it. I have a reputation to protect, and if my parents, especially my mom, ever knew what I was doing outside of that crowd I'd be in serious trouble. You actually don't understand how serious. Anyway, I don't see you telling the other students how much you care about people. You come across as aloof and tough."

"I was pretty tough tonight."

"How so?"

"I got sick of my parents running me down for babysitting instead of being a law clerk. So, I fed them a line of bull that shut them up."

Dawn laughed. "Excellent."

I ran my fingers through my hair to comb it, and shrugged, giving her my best cooled-out look. "Dawn, we both do a great deal of acting at school. I can't be myself around the other students. If I played the sweet, sensitive around the dudes at school I'd never hear the end of that. People would use it against me. With you I can be myself, sort of. You're the prettiest, most special girl I know. I...I love you. If we were a few years older, I'd ask you to marry me."

Dawn blushed. "You'd what? Oh my...I can't believe you just said that."

I turned and started walking away. "Forget it. I'm sorry I said it. I was letting my heart speak." I shrugged, realizing it was stupid of me to share my emotions.

Dawn walked over to me and turned me around gently. She

had tears in her eyes, and her face looked softer somehow. "Francis" she spoke my real name softly, "if I was a few years older, I would accept that offer."

We joined hands and walked to the park silently. Every so often Dawn looked up at me and then looked away. I noticed how much brighter the moon looked, how beautifully the trees shimmered beneath the streetlamps. We walked into the park and started along the garden paths.

Dawn stopped and turned to look at me. "Once we're back in school, I'm going to quit being who everyone expects me to be. We can sit together at lunch, and I'm going to try art class. I'm not that good at it, but I'll try. If Heather, or Faye, or Hope, or any of them ask about this diamond ring, I'll tell them you gave it to me. I will."

I shook my head. "You amaze me. I appreciate it, but not if you are going to end up in serious trouble. We can keep our relationship to ourselves if you'd rather. I don't mind."

Dawn and I kissed. She held me in an embrace for a few minutes, her ear pressed to my heart. I ran my hands over the tight denim on the rear of her jeans and enjoyed the moment. In the distance I heard a familiar voice.

"I know this research means a great deal to you, Shemmy, but the article needs to be written and finished. If we don't get it together and peer reviewed, then we can't raise the grant money for more housing." A man with a basso profundo voice sounded agitated.

The voice of Top Cat responded, "I understand this. Like I stated, I recently met some young people who put a different spin on these matters. Something is happening that I didn't count on. There is something far more complex at play than just urban youth who have been rejected and abandoned. There is something that may turn our paper in a direction that is more far reaching."

"Explain that." The deep voice demanded.

"There are children who are from the upper end of the socioeconomic ladder. I don't know how many are involved, but I have met at last two who are teenagers and a child who I suspect is the brother of one of them. That child, while he may be four or five, is already taking part in the changes occurring. Something larger than our original paper is happening in this area. I sense something even bigger may occur if we wait." Top Cat sounded more erudite and less hip than I had previously noticed.

Dawn and I sat on a bench twenty feet away and waited for the second man to depart. We stood and held hands, walking by Top Cat as if we didn't notice him.

"What's up, dudes?" Top Cat called after us. "You're both out pretty late. Where's your kid brother, man?"

Dawn and I turned around. "He isn't my brother; I babysit for him. What's happening with you? We didn't want to interrupt your conversation." I shrugged.

"Oh, you heard that?"

Dawn nodded, "Some of it. What was that guy talking about?"

Top Cat paused and scratched his chin, "I can't tell you. Not yet. It's complicated. Not everything in life is as it appears."

"I understand that. Dawn and I were talking about that very thing earlier. We'll let it go. Forget about it." I held Dawn closer. "We have to get going, but we'll be around tomorrow."

Dawn and I walked through the park and stopped suddenly. There was music playing. Not music like Top Cat played, or like Get Lost Jimmy played. This was grittier, louder, with distinct punk overtones.

"Who is that?" I asked Dawn.

"Probably some of the guys who live over there. There's a small group of guys who call themselves Ryan Coke. They have a band that sometimes plays shows to make a few bucks. I don't know them that well, but we have a few mutual friends who play for the Cunning Stunts."

I shook my head. "You're friends with The Stunners?"

Dawn laughed. "I dare you to call any of them The Stunners when they're around. Tough or not, you'll get your ass handed back to you. Did you know that the city used to have concerts in this park?"

"I didn't know that. You mean like. Classical and Jazz?"

Dawn laughed, "Well, yeah. But, from what Cricket and Panda told me there were also punk concerts and straight rock concerts."

"Cricket and Panda? You mean the lead guitarist and bassist for The Cunning Stunts?"

"Only people I know with those names. Yeah. They live in one of the camps around here during the summer. I think they have a camper somewhere in winter and when they tour. I got to know them a few months ago when I was looking for some hash I heard was available."

"That band, Ryan Coke, play great. I'm enjoying this sound. I knew the stun...The Cunning Stunts were local, but I didn't know they were homeless. I bought one of their tapes a few months ago. From a guy at school." I moved involuntarily to the sounds emanating from the woods.

"Yeah, I agree. They're awesome." Dawn danced with me. "I don't think all the girls are homeless, just Cricket and Panda."

"I wish they could still play in the park."

"The concerts were banned in the park a while back and

especially rock concerts. I don't know why exactly."

"We should ask Top Cat tomorrow. Or Jimmy. Maybe Hetty knows. One thing for sure, adults suck. Except them. So far. They seem pretty cool."

"They do. Want to go get some ice cream, or a sandwich?" Dawn took my hand, and we kept walking.

"We could get an ice cream sandwich," I gave her a pat on the butt.

"I was thinking about maybe a hot fudge sundae. Then I need to get home."

"Yeah, me too. I wish I didn't. I could stay up all night enjoying your company."

We exited the park and headed to a corner ice cream shop. I ordered and paid for a Hot Fudge Bonanza with two spoons. Dawn and I ate and gazed at each other. Afterward I took her home and returned to my house. I was feeling some kind of way, but I couldn't put the feelings to words.

CHAPTER FOURTEEN

I woke early and put on my headphones. I had purchased a CD of a local punk band, "Sonic Belch," recently, and their sound was a good way to greet the dawn.

After a shower and shave, I noticed that the clock read a quarter past six. I dressed and walked silent and stealthy down the stairs. I had no desire to wake my parents or Mrs. Ferrigno. As it turned out, my father was awake and working on some legal briefs.

"Good morning, father. I hope I didn't wake you. I couldn't sleep." I poured orange juice and put a bagel in the toaster.

"Not at all. I have quite a caseload, and I was up working on part of it. Anything the matter that you should be up this early?"

I paused, looking for some neutral grounds of discussion. My sex life and my thoughts about civil justice were not subjects I felt comfortable bringing to the fore; albeit they were why I was unable to sleep. "I was thinking about some articles I researched for a paper in school last term. It has to do with a legal matter, but it might not be one with which you are familiar."

"Try me, son." My father freshened his coffee and poured me a mug.

I put cream cheese and nova-lox on my bagel and turned my chair to face him. "There was this girl, in nineteen and seventy-nine, she was my age. She opened fire on an elementary school across the street from her house in San Diego I believe it was."

"You are referring to Brenda Ann Spencer?" My father's eyes lit up slightly. "I was a year out of law school when that occurred. I know the story, although I am not familiar with the finer details of the case."

"I started researching the articles because she was only a bit older than me. She was an outcast from all I read, and a bit mentally disturbed. It sounded as if her lawyers never brought these matters up in court. I wondered if she would have received a lesser sentence had they done so."

"Ah! The McNaghten rule. Affirmative insanity defense is a tricky one, even in a pink state like California. I understand your contention, son, and yes as a defense lawyer I would have tried to go with it. From what I understand she was clearly not mentally competent."

"I wonder sometimes about certain students at my school. They're bullied, harassed, and looked down upon by most teachers. The other students either ostracize them or bully them as well. I wonder that more students don't flip that switch in their brain and open a free fire zone."

My father grinned at me and sipped his coffee. "For a young man who shows almost no interest in pursuing the law as a career, you certainly are skilled with the proper thinking. I do wish that you would consider working in my firm next summer."

"We'll see. I might. Especially if there is anyone who is a defense attorney and works with the under-privileged."

"Not in my firm there isn't. If you are determined to take the side of the liberals, and I can't say as I understand why that is the case, I could direct you to some people. I don't much care for the ACLU, but you might like their causes. There are other pink organizations as well whom you might consider."

I realized that the conversation was heading into dangerous territory, so I finished my breakfast in silence. I rinsed my glass, mug, and plate, and put them in the dishwasher.

"I'll be leaving shortly. I'm heading to the gym and maybe to a museum. I'll clean my room before I head out." I walked toward the kitchen door.

"It would make your mother happy if you did that." My father had already resumed his legal briefs.

An hour later I left and walked to Dawn's. I stopped at a pay phone on the way and called her to let her know I was coming. When I arrived, she was ready to work out. We walked toward the fitness center holding hands.

"What's wrong, Cyrus?" Dawn and I crossed the street and headed south.

"Wrong?" I shrugged.

"You look troubled." Dawn side-hugged me.

"I wasn't aware it showed. Yeah, I have a lot on my mind."

We walked in silence a bit. I listened to the birds, watched the clouds drift, and tried to put to words the deep sense of weltschmerz and ennui that was enveloping me.

"So, what's going on?" Dawn asked.

"There's a lot going on. I'm finding myself more in love with each breath I take. I never expected that to happen, and certainly not between us. I don't want to lose what we have, but I keep thinking it will end and we'll go back to who we were before."

Dawn smiled softly. "That won't happen. Not if we don't let

it. I love you, too. I mean I can't think of anything else other than being with you most of the time. Want to know something crazy embarrassing?"

"Sure."

"Promise you won't laugh at me?"

"I promise."

Dawn looked away and blushed. "I have a notebook and I write in it, over and over, Dawn Meredith Ahriman."

I chuckled. "I'm not laughing at you. I understand how you feel."

"So, what else is wrong?" Dawn asked.

"Like I said I'm afraid this is all going to end. Even if it doesn't, I'm scared I'll become like my father. I fear taking you for granted and ignoring you like he does my mother. Or I fear becoming a nasty hurtful person like my mother. I don't want to ever be like them."

"You won't. I'm not going to be like my parents either. We can be different. We already are."

"I guess. Also," we approached the entrance to the fitness center, "I think about the other teens in the park. I think about the homeless adults. Maybe they want concerts in the park. Maybe the members of Ryan Coke and The Cunning Stunts want to be allowed to play their music for others in the park without being harassed. I don't know why I care, though. I have money, a nice home, you. Why do I care so much about the homeless?"

"I don't know. Why do you?"

"I guess because it's unfair. They have no one to depend on, no one to trust. They got shafted by society, and now they get shafted again. They didn't ask to live in the park, that's for damned sure. If they want concerts, why shouldn't they have them?"

Dawn smiled at me. "I agree. You think we should do something about that?"

I thought for a few minutes. "You mean like arrange for some bands to play? I was listening to Sonic Belch this morning. I bet we could get them to play. You know some members of The Cunning Stunts. We could ask Jamie from Rabid Flatulence if they'd perform. Maybe get the Kung Fools."

"I used to score from Luther who plays bass for The Kung Fools. He was telling me that there's a band led by his friend Dimitris. They call themselves Mosh Potatoes."

I laughed, "That's a ludicrous name for a band, but whatever. We can include them, too."

I signed in and listed Dawn as my guest. She nodded. "I think Sonic Belch is a bit sophomoric, myself, but we can ask them. I wish Eight Ball was still touring. I'd write them a fan letter and ask them to headline."

"Let's think about this some more. We have the rest of the summer."

"Feeling better?"

"Much."

As Dawn and I approached the treadmills a sense of calm enveloped me. Dawn and I had found our next cause. Something told me that it would be spectacular.

CHAPTER FIFTEEN

Four days later Ms. Cramer called. I was eating breakfast and watching *The Price is Right* with Mrs. Ferrigno.

"Hello. Ahriman residence." I answered after three rings.

"Cyrus? This is Lynn Cramer. I needed to inform you that Jeremiah has been ill. I'm taking him to his doctor, and he will need three days to recuperate. I understand that this isn't anything you caused, and I will pay you something for the inconvenience of losing a few days employment."

I had grown accustomed to caring for Jack, but three days off meant more time alone with Dawn. Also, I was going to make money for taking the time off. It was a sweet deal.

"Jeremiah seemed a bit lethargic the past two days, I must admit. I did stop and get him a bowl of chicken soup the other afternoon. He ate it with a glass of soda water."

"That's fine, Cyrus. This isn't anything you caused. Jeremiah gets sick sometimes. He has inner ear problems. I'll let you go, and I'll see you in a few days."

I called Dawn to let her know. She sounded pleased. "If you want, I can tell my parents I'm spending the night at Heather's. You do the same thing with your parents. We can go to this spot I know in the woods and see what develops.

"Sounds great. Maybe we can get a mushroom pizza and split it."

Dawn giggled, "That's the idea. Maybe a few brownies as well."

I finished breakfast and took a hot shower. I dressed in a loose t-shirt and jeans. I had no idea what mushrooms would do to me, but Dawn made the experience sound like something I needed to try.

When I informed my parents that I might be staying over at a friend's house for a day or two, they informed me that they were going out of town for four days to attend a conference for my father's law firm. My mother pointed out several times that if I had accepted their advice about my future law career, I could travel to Florida with them and enjoy the resort at which they were lodging. I didn't mention that I had far more interesting plans.

Mrs. Ferrigno was taking two days off to attend her niece's wedding, and therefore I had my house to myself. The set up was perfect, and I called Dawn again to let her know what was going on.

Two hours later I bid my parents farewell, and an hour after that Dawn arrived. We carried her backpack upstairs to my room and sat on the floor facing each other.

"I've only tripped once before, Cyrus. I only took a micro-dose, and it wasn't much. It enhanced the pot I had smoked is all. I know a place in the woods where we can trip and be safe while still having some girls I know nearby if we need help." Dawn held my hands.

"Help with what? Is this something dangerous?" I asked.

"No. It shouldn't be. If you go into it nervous and anxious it might not be as enjoyable, but if you relax and trust yourself and me, then it should be exhilarating and open you to deeper artistic expression. Anyway, that's my understanding of it from McKenna and Leary."

"Is what I'm wearing OK?"

"It's perfect. You don't want your movement inhibited and you don't want to feel confined. I was thinking that maybe we could go get some salad or something and then take a micro-dose to start. I think that they're showing *The Muppet Movie* at the afternoon matinee. That would be a spectacular way to start. Afterward we can go to the area I mentioned and take a regular dose. I want to see what happens, and I want to see with you."

Dawn stood. I grabbed my notebook and sketch pad. I placed them in my pack and stood as well. We walked to a bus stop near the park and caught an uptown to a café that was near the country club. Dawn and I each ordered a smoked Gouda grilled cheese panino and a strawberry spinach salad with candied pecans, feta, and balsamic vinaigrette. Washed down with mineral water, it was worth the slightly higher than usual price.

After lunch we caught the bus toward the theater. Dawn and I ducked into an area behind an office building. We smoked two bowls of pot, and each ate a mushroom stem. We purchased our tickets and sat in the darkened theater with our Cokes. Inside of fifteen minutes I was experiencing a more intense effect than I had previously found while smoking out. By that time, I knew well the relaxing effects of THC, but I had never felt fused to my seat. I was alert, but my body felt so comfortable in the theater chair that moving around seemed ludicrous.

The movie started and the colors were brighter and more vivid than I recalled them being in prior viewings. Even better was that I felt intellectually and cosmically aware. *The*

Muppet Movie, a movie aimed at kids, held deeper and far more complex nuance than I remembered. Beyond its whimsy, its achievements in special effects, and its cultural significance, it was, at its essence, a tale of one's dreams coming true. I was saturated with optimism that felt like a breath of fresh air when pondering a frequently harsh reality that inundated every second of my life.

After the movie we stepped from the dim environment of the theater into the glaring, bright sunlight of the afternoon. The warmth of the sun on my face was delicious. The extreme aura-like radiance surrounding everyone, and everything was jarring. I wasn't altogether certain that my imagination wasn't causing the effect.

"That movie is so deep. And those seats were so comfortable." I held Dawn's hand and floated through the after-movie crowds.

Dawn giggled. "Yeah, I totally agree. The guy I bought from, Humberto, said he crossed Northern Lights with G13. Must admit that it has serious couch lock elements. I'm thirsty. Let's go get some coffee or something."

As we wandered the surrounding neighborhoods, I began to notice a certain aesthetic beauty in the architecture. "I wish I lived in some of these houses. I mean, mine is nice, but the ranch style architecture can't beat some of this stuff."

Dawn stood holding my hand as we looked up at the Queen Anne turrets on a house across the street. "I love that style. Those towers always remind me of a castle."

"Me, too. I think it's the sort of place Kermit might build for Piggy, or Gonzo would climb to rescue Camilla."

Dawn giggled more, "Gonzo?"

"Yeah. I felt something during the movie. Gonzo, whatever

108

he is, he's not just a sadomasochistic, chicken-loving daredevil whose place in the universe is all but ambiguous. I always thought that before, and I am certain most see him that way. This time around, maybe it's because of what we ate, I realized that he's really a somewhat lonely soul whose uniqueness is as much of a blessing as it is a curse. I can relate to that on a deep level."

"Interesting. I see your point." Dawn turned and hugged me. "That stem you ate is a mushroom called a blue meanie. We'll have more later on."

We walked further, and as the effects wore down a bit, we settled for a bakery that had iced coffee and apple strudel. Dawn ate, and I began writing a poem that came to me.

When the stare begins to dissolve time

The eyes become marbles reflecting

Moments of bliss before the fall.

Dancing, twirling spirals of light,

The progressing now replaces all thought.

Logic and reason trap us in suffocating cellars

The mind cannot unlock.

The now embraces soul-level darkness.

I handed my notebook to Dawn, and she read. "Cyrus, you have got to submit this somewhere. You're wildly deep and cosmic.

I'd be afraid to do that. I'm not sure anyone would understand my writings. I'm not sure I do. It's like with my art. I draw what I see, and I write what comes to me, but others find more than I realize I put out there. What if they laugh at me? What if they hate my work?"

"What if they don't?" Dawn took a napkin and wiped crumbs from her mouth. "What if this is your way to tell the world something they need to know?"

I thought about that as we walked toward the woods. Evening was approaching as Dawn introduced me to two girls, I had neither met nor seen around school. One was named Alicia. She was of medium height, curvy, with blonde hair done in braids. Next to her was her girlfriend, Robyn, who was taller than me by three inches, had long raven-black hair, and resembled Morticia Addams.

"Cyrus, I reserved an area in the woods for us where no one will come around unless we shout out for them. Robyn and Alicia are going to be nearby, but not too near. If they sense our trip is going bad, they'll step in and guide us back, but that's unlikely."

"Pleasure to meet you, and thank you, I guess. I've never done this before. I have no preconceptions here. I hope it helps me become more artistically open."

Robin smiled a calming and soothing smile. "It's better that way. It will help you as an artist. It helps me, anyway."

Dawn and I walked a bit further into the woods, and suddenly we were in a small area surrounded by a copse of pines. Someone had laid out quilts and blankets. The area above was open, but otherwise we were secluded.

Dawn opened the baggie and we each ate two caps and a stem. We smoked a bowl of pot and sat facing each other holding hands. At first nothing happened except that I felt more stoned than ever. After a half hour I noticed that the trees were melting around us. Or rather they were swaying and dancing. It was somewhere between a horror movie and Fantasia.

I took Dawn by the hands, and we stood. She and I tried to dance in the motion of the trees, but we ended up falling all over each other. I felt myself melting into the ground as I shifted into a viscous form.

We lay there on the quilts and blankets, and I pulled off my t-shirt. The material was melting into my skin, or anyway I thought it was. Dawn followed suit, and we lay there together bare chested.

Dawn curled up in my arms. "You're part of my soul now, Cyrus. Our innermost beings are eternally fused, and our two bodies have become one. We are inseparable."

She felt very small and delicate, and I sensed a need to keep her safe. "I should morph into something strong and protective. I'll become your protective cloak."

"Protect me forever, my lord. I am yours to do with as you please, so long as you protect me. I belong to you and you to me."

Snuggling together turned into touching each other in various spots as we removed more items of clothing piece by piece. It felt totally amazing to touch another human while tripping. Actual intercourse seemed impossible, simply because it would have been hard to get my body to move in the way it would have to. Everything felt like we were moving in slow motion.

I was fingering Dawn and she was stroking me. My whole body started to glow and pulsate, to vibrate with sexual energy, which eventually built up into this powerful, raw, sexual force. I started to rock my body and orgasm. Dawn had her legs up, head back, and was moaning softly.

Even the feel of the ground, or the bark on the trees, was immensely erotic. Standing was virtually impossible because it was so stimulating that I'd have to stop to orgasm. I was discovering possibilities in this crazy, sexy plane of existence to which we had journeyed.

Dawn moaned "I want all of your aura inside of me."

I was barely moving, just holding on as long as I could before the explosion. I didn't feel guilty or ashamed, I felt like Dawn's and my aura and essence were fusing. In a beam of light from the setting sun, I held her close, looked at her, and spoke her full name. She was beautiful like a Greek goddess.

By that point I was nearing the end of the peak and we had just had our moment. It felt like pure ecstasy like the most love any human could ever give and receive. It was like we were sending and receiving, more like exchanging, our energy through our lips and bodies. Each movement was so fluid and felt natural like we were wild animals, and it was instinct. I smelled her perfume; reminiscent of a childhood memory which I could not figure out exactly what it was. I kept smelling it and suddenly I experienced Synesthesia. I was physically feeling the scent of her on my chest. It felt like my chest and arms were shape shifting, kind of wavy, and as difficult to explain to one who has not experienced it as it was for me to understand synesthesia before feeling this.

As the energy subsided, and I found my moorings, I reached into my pack for my sketchpad. I began drawing what I was seeing and feeling. I sketched Dawn as a tree nymph, and then as a single entity fused with the quilt beneath her. I was in the middle of a drawing when I saw her turn and lean into a tree.

I grabbed Dawn before she fell, and as I held her hair back, she threw up. She buckled to her knees and vomited until she was empty. Then it was my turn, and I got equally ill. The sensation of vomiting was terrifying. I felt as if unseen elements were shoving their fingers down my gullet and forcing me to heave even when I was empty.

We cleaned our faces as best we could, using some discarded towels. After we had cleaned up, we got dressed. My watch told me we had been in the park for four hours. It was dark as we walked back toward the paths and headed to my house. The effects of the mushrooms were still present, but they were muted. I began to question the sensibility of using psychonautic means to enhance a deeper creativity.

After we entered my house and made sure everything was locked up, we headed upstairs and took a hot shower. Dawn changed into a long t-shirt and crawled into my bed. I put on boxers and climbed in beside her. We fell asleep in each other's arms.

The effects of the mushrooms were still working on my system, for I began to have a wild dream. A pink dragon flew through the walls and scooped me onto his back. I looked to my left and a bit in front, and Dawn was riding like Lady Godiva atop a blue dragon. She spurred it on, and I spotted Jack Flash ahead of us both. His dragon was red and purple, and he was moving with increasing speed. Jack was dressed in his pajamas. I looked down and saw that I was wearing my best suit and tie. It made no sense.

I spurred on my dragon and overtook Dawn with a quick smack to her behind as I passed. I managed to catch up with Jack, but he whispered something to his dragoon, and they flew faster yet. Jack won the race, and Dawn and I were thrown from our dragons. We were forced to prostrate ourselves and declare Jack the victor. In the distance a bell was ringing.

I sat up and turned off my alarm. I returned to snuggling with Dawn who was still out cold. I couldn't fall back asleep, and instead lay thinking. The effects of mushrooms were weird, and in some ways frightening. They left me confused more than they made me aware. Pot relaxed me, but mushrooms made me sick. I decided that whatever creative benefits I got from tripping, the downside outweighed the plusses. I was done with that experiment. I hoped that Dawn agreed.

CHAPTER SIXTEEN

A few days later, Dawn sat on the curb at the end of the block as I approached The Cramer's. It was eight in the morning. Our plan was for her to wait twenty minutes and then walk by the house. If Ms. Cramer had left, I would hang a red bandana from the doorknob.

Over the previous three days we had discussed every pro and con of taking psychonautic drugs. We agreed that we weren't ready for them, and that we might never be ready for them. It had taken a full day of recuperation just to feel normal again. We both understood that some writers and philosophers believed in the underlying power of tripping, but something wasn't working for us. We had no access to the authors other than through their writings, and that was a problem that we couldn't surmount.

While Dawn waited, I approached the Cramer house and noticed that there was no car in the driveway. I knocked, and Jack peeked out through a curtain. He waved and came to open the door.

"Mommy had to leave fast. She said that she left you something in the kitchen." Jack returned to his spot in front of the TV. He looked distracted, like something was bothering him.

115

I walked into the kitchen and found an envelope on the table. Inside was instructions, a house key, and $200.00 for expenses. I pocketed the key, put the money in my wallet, and went to sit with Jack.

"Everything OK, buddy?"

"Yes. I'm fine." He stared at the TV.

"You sure? You look sad."

"I'm fine. Mommy said I talk too much and ask too many questions. So, I'm being quiet."

I nodded and sat beside him.

"Where's that girl?" Jack looked at me. "Didn't she come?"

"Oh sh...oot!" I hopped up and opened the door. Dawn was walking by. I waved her in.

"Sorry. I completely forgot the plan after I arrived. Ms. Cramer was already gone, and I got to talking to Jack."

Dawn giggled. "You dork!" She set her pack down and looked at Jack. "Hey, kid. Excited for our four days of adventure?"

Jack stood up and snarled at her, "I'm not a kid. I'm a big boy!"

Dawn took a step back. "I'm sorry. I forgot."

"Yeah?" Jack growled. "Well don't forget again, got it?"

I was shocked. "Jack, what's wrong? She was just being friendly."

"Nothing. I can't talk about it."

I looked at Dawn. She shrugged at me. I scooped Jack up and sat him in my lap. He leaned against me and sighed. I reflected on the fact that he was a bright kid for five years old, but that it was clear he held secrets in his heart and head. I was trying to figure out how to get him to open up about what was troubling him when Dawn suddenly walked to the door.

"I'm going to leave you both alone for a bit. I'll be back in an hour." Dawn left and I sat watching TV with Jack.

As a cartoon came on, I cleared my throat. "So, we have a few days together? What would you like to do that you don't get to do when you have to be Jeremiah?"

Jack looked up at me and smiled. "I don't know. What can we do? We can go to the park. What else?"

I rubbed my chin. "Want to go to the movies again? Maybe go to the amusement park on the other side of town? We could go to the airport and watch planes take off, maybe. Ever been bowling? We could invite some of your school friends over and play games."

"The movies sound like fun. I've only been to the amusement park once, but now I never get to go. I've never seen planes taking off, only the ones flying up in the sky. I don't know how to bowl. And you're my only friend, Cyrus. You and Dawn. I mean Top Cat is and Get Lost Jimmy and Uncle Don. Mommy won't let me invite kids from school over. She doesn't like me going to their homes either."

I processed the last bit of information and couldn't formulate an adequate reply. Jack and I continued watch TV, and forty-five minutes later Dawn knocked on the door. She had multiple shopping bags full of snack cakes, hotdogs, hamburger, buns, chips, chocolate, and soda pop.

"Hey Jack, want to help me put this stuff away and later we can cook some lunch?" Dawn grinned.

"I'm not allowed to cook. If I touch the stove without asking, I get smacked." Jack scooted off of my lap and stood. "I'm sorry I got angry with you earlier." He hugged Dawn.

Dawn knelt down. "You're a big boy, you can learn to cook. Just don't tell anyone. Like with you being Jack Flash."

She and Jack walked into the kitchen and began rustling about.

I grabbed the paper and looked at what movies were playing that evening. I also checked on the hours for the amusement park, and the schedules for the busses. Dawn and Jack returned to the living room. We watched TV until eleven. For lunch they made us chili cheese hotdogs and chips. Dawn handed me a plate and returned to fetch hers.

I took a bite, chewed, swallowed, and pointed at the paper. "I saw that there's a Chris Makepeace double feature tonight. *Meatballs* and *My Bodyguard*. You two interested?"

Dawn nodded, "That sounds cool. Maybe we can get ice cream afterward."

"I need one of those." Jack stated solemnly.

"One of what? An ice cream?" I asked.

"No, a bodyguard."

Dawn and I looked at each other. She softened her voice, "Why does Jack Flash need a bodyguard? He's a superhero. He saves the planet."

Jack shrugged, "I just do. Sometimes the bad guys are really mean."

I finished my hotdogs. "Care to tell me more about that, buddy?"

"I can't. I'm just glad that you and Dawn are here for four days. It'll be fun."

Dawn and I did the dishes while Jack ran up to his room and began looking for an outfit to wear to the movies. When we came back to the living room, Jack was watching TV again. He had on his overalls, his baseball cap, and a blue t-shirt."

"When does the movie start?" Jack asked.

"The paper says the first one is at six. We can go to the park first if you want, or whatever you feel like."

"I bet Top Cat is at the park. We could invite him to the

movies." Jack bounced up and down.

Dawn and I freshened up, and we headed out the door. Jack was more hyper than he had been, and genuinely looked pleased to be spending time with us. As we approached the benches where we usually sat, Top Cat was playing a series of fifties tunes while people danced. Between tunes the audience tossed money into his guitar case.

"Hey, dudes. What's happening? I'm having a pretty good day here. We have a regular National Bandstand going." Top Cat started in on "Rock 'n' Roll is Here to Stay."

Dawn scooped up Jack and danced with him. I danced beside them, although I wasn't as good at it as Dawn. After the crowds cleared a bit and Top Cat counted his money, I sat beside him with Jack on my lap. Dawn sat beside me.

"I was thinking about something earlier, TC. Dawn and I were talking about maybe getting some of the local bands together to play a concert in the park. You interested in playing?"

Top Cat shook his head. "Count me out on that one. It's a great idea, but you don't understand the situation. Protesting to get bratwursts is one thing, but this idea of yours is way beyond that. There's a reason why the city banned the concerts. You try to arrange that without cutting though a lot of red tape, and you'll end up in more trouble than you can handle. Even with the red tape you'll lose."

"What are you taping? And why are you using red tape?" Jack asked.

Top Cat chuckled. "Red tape just means a lot of governmental and bureaucratic regulations."

"Oh." Jack gave him a blank stare.

"Rules, Jack. It means we have to ask a lot of people who make rules. People who will say no even if we ask nicely." Dawn sighed.

"Why is the tape red?"

Top Cat cleared his throat. "It is generally believed that the term red tape originated with the Spanish administration of Charles the fifth in the early sixteenth century. He started to use red tape in an effort to modernize the administration that was running his vast empire. The red tape was used to bind the most important administrative dossiers that required immediate discussion and separate them from issues that were treated in a more ordinary way. The more ordinary documents were bound with string."

"Oh." Jack shrugged.

Dawn, Jack, and I walked toward the playground and Jack sat on the swings. I pondered what Top Cat had said. My stomach felt tight, and my heartrate increased.

"Dammit," I looked at Dawn. "Why do adults always stand in the way of freedom? Why can't they just let us make the world better, or our corner of it anyway?"

Dawn shrugged, "I have no idea, Cyrus." She leaned against me, "I think it's still a good idea. Might take a week or two for us to arrange, but we should do it."

An hour later the three of us boarded a cross-town bus. We paid half price for Jack because he was five, and Dawn and I showed our student passes. Jack sat on Dawn's lap and closed his eyes. I watched him leaning his head on her chest, and for a moment imagined us as a family. It was an interesting fantasy, but I quickly dismissed it. Dawn and I were falling in love, but I was nowhere near ready to be a father and she wasn't ready to be a mother.

I began thinking about my American history class at VHI the past year. Only a century earlier there had been people our age marrying and starting families. It wasn't as usual as it had been a century before that, but it wasn't unheard of. Even in the late thirties or early forties, Loretta Lynn had married at fourteen and had kids by the age of fifteen. So, the fantasy wasn't out of bounds, but the cases I recalled were all lower income bracket and blue collar. Dawn and I didn't fit into that paradigm. I was still certain that Dawn and I could make a better go of it than our parents.

I looked out the window of the bus and noticed the area through which we were riding. It was rather blue collar. There were factories, and garages, and the sort of businesses that catered to my parents and Dawn's when they needed labor done. I felt my muscles tighten as groups boarded, loud and boisterous, and sat near us. The feelings aroused irritated me. I disliked my parents' notions about those whose socioeconomic status was below ours, but I was reacting in a similar manner. There was no need for that. I looked at Dawn and Jack and they weren't showing any signs of concern. That caused me to feel more agitated.

I was beating myself up mentally for being elitist and prejudiced when the bus pulled up a half of a block away from the amusement park. We disembarked, and I put Jack on my shoulders. He waved at everyone as we walked. Once we reached the entrance, I lowered Jack and paid to get bands that let us ride the rides for free. I told the lady at the ticket booth that Jack was four, so he got in for free, but I made certain that he didn't hear me say it.

Our first stop was the bumper cars. I climbed into a car with Jack sitting beside me. Dawn climbed into a second car. As the ride commenced, we spotted a couple in their car at the edge of the ride. The couple was sharing a kiss when I aimed directly for the front of their car. Dawn was aiming for the rear. We timed it perfectly and simultaneously slammed into them. The guy sat bolt upright and glared at us, but we were already riding away laughing.

Jack and I had several head on collisions with Dawn, and we helped her T-bone numerous other riders. The line was short, so we rode a second time before heading to the arcade. Jack was energized by the ride and couldn't stand still. Dawn took him by the hand so that we didn't lose him in the crowds.

I traded cash for tokens, and we played video games. Jack wasn't as good as me and Dawn at the games, and he eventually started watching us play. We gravitated to some carney games, and I began playing one that involved tossing balls in trash cans with lids that opened and closed at haphazard intervals. I continued trading up my prizes until I won a giant stuffed Flamingo for Dawn and a baseball cap with the name of the park on it for Jack.

We rode the carousel a few times and took Jack to enjoy a number of children's rides. We finished the afternoon by riding in the teacups. Jack loved them.

"Faster! Faster! Come on, Cyrus and Dawn, we have to turn the wheel more, so we spin even faster."

Dawn and I laughed as the teacup spun wildly. Everything was out of control – if only I had known just how much so.

A couple hours later we exited and headed to a diner. It was four in the afternoon, and we were ready for the movies. The diner was mid-way between the park and our side of town. We rode the bus and climbed off before walking three blocks.

"I want French fries," Jack smiled up at me.

"Can do," I replied.

Dawn walked us to a booth and asked Jack if he wanted a

booster seat.

Jack stuck out his tongue, "I'm not a baby. I can sit in the seat same as you and Cyrus. Girls!"

"Boys!" Dawn giggled Jack giggled back.

Our waitress appeared. I looked her up and down, smiled at her, and said we were ready to order. Dawn kicked me under the table, and I looked down at my menu.

"I'll take a cheeseburger, fries, and a cup of coffee." I put down my menu.

Jack looked at me and Dawn. "Can I get these chili and cheese fries?"

Dawn nodded. "He'll take the small chili and cheese fries, and a Coke. I'll have a cheeseburger too, fries, and a Coke."

The waitress walked away, and I watched her behind twitch out of the corner of my eye. Dawn cleared her throat.

"Cyrus, I'm sitting right here. No need to let your eyes rove to greener pasture."

"Excuse you? You have it all over any woman in this place. You know that. I admit that maybe I have a type, but it's just how men are. We like to look and imagine. I admit that she's a lentiginous pyrrhotist of diminutive proportions, but I'll take reality over fantasy any day."

Jack was looking at us and trying to follow our conversation. "What is she?"

"She's a short redhead with freckles."

"Then why didn't you say that?" Jack asked.

Dawn laughed. "Yeah, Cyrus, why didn't you just say that?"

I stuck my tongue out at Dawn and looked at Jack. "It's good to have a broad vocabulary. If you want to build one, then you have to use bigger words from time to time."

"Oh." Jack shrugged. "So, what were you imagining about

her, Cyrus?"

"You don't need to know, Jack. I mean that. It isn't about being too little. It's something you'll understand in six or seven years."

"Oh," Jack giggled. "You like that girl who took our order."

Dawn almost choked on her glass of water and began to laugh. "You're pretty smart for a five-year-old."

Jack suddenly looked down, his mood growing dark again. "I think I'm too smart sometimes. Mommy says so, anyway."

I glanced at Dawn who shrugged. "Jack," I tried to sound gentle, "is something bothering you? Did something happen the past few days?"

"No. Nothing that I can talk about. I had to go to a doctor and get a bunch of shots. Some of them were in my butt and they hurt. Mommy said that we might be moving somewhere else at the end of the summer. I don't know where, but it's very far south."

The sodas came and my coffee. I put the matter aside for later. Dawn ruffled Jack's hair, and he growled playfully.

"Don't muss up my hair." Jack pouted.

"You excited to see the movies?"

Jack was suddenly bubbly again. "Yeah. I love going to the movies. I love you and Cyrus. I wish we could play forever."

The food came and we began to eat. I sat thinking about how bright Jack was and trying to figure out what was bothering him. Something in the back of my mind told me that there was a problem I wasn't seeing, but I couldn't pull the thought to the front portion of my brain.

CHAPTER SEVENTEEN

We boarded the bus at five, and Jack took a nap in my lap as we rode back across town. Dawn took Jack and carried him as we disembarked near the theater. It was almost six, and I spotted a Port-o-Pot on a corner near a construction site.

"Hey, we can't really light up out here, and with Jack it'd be really tough anyway. You think if we each stepped inside there, we could have a few tokes?" I whispered.

Dawn nodded and slipped the pipe and bag of buds into my hand. I entered the foul smelling, fetid chamber and loaded the bowl. I smoked four good hits and stepped out. After taking Jack from Dawn, she entered the portable bathroom and exited five minutes later. Jack was just waking up from his nap.

We paid for our tickets, purchased sodas, and found seats. The theater was fairly crowded for a matinee, and the pot was having a strong effect. I looked at Jack and wondered whether Dawn and I were neglecting our responsibilities by getting stoned while babysitting. The moral questions were short lived as the movie started.

Meatballs was one of my favorite summer movies. It had come out before I was old enough to enjoy movies in the theater, but I had seen it numerous times over the years. It was actually a

Bill Murray vehicle, and it was his comedic spontaneity that gave the movie its greatness. Chris Makepeace, however, was a perfect foil to Murray, and was no slouch as a semi-serious actor.

Murray had appeared in several other movies that I thought of as comedy classics. He was a riot, up there with Robin Williams, John Belushi, and Eddie Murphy. In *Meatballs*, however, Murray demonstrated a rare example of onscreen dramatic tenderness.

His scenes with the shy Rudy, portrayed by Makepeace, gave the film something extra. The duo clowned around, but it was evident they cared for each other. Watching how Rudy needed, Murray's Tripper, and how they helped each other grow made me think about Jack. I was sort of a mentor to him in the same way Murray was to Makepeace.

I couldn't see in the dark of the theater to write down my musings, but I made a mental note to do so later. I figured that Mr. K. might have something to say about my thoughts. I also wondered if I could flesh my thoughts out and submit them as an essay in English class the following term.

After the first movie, there was an intermission. We took the opportunity to use the restrooms and refresh our drinks. Jack was still going strong and kept bubbling about how Rudy won the race at the end of the film. Once we were seated again, *My Bodyguard* started.

I had seen *My Bodyguard* a couple of times, and it was much more of a vehicle for Makepeace. The story was more down-to-earth than was *Meatballs.* Granted that the violence throughout, and the thrilling final fight, were a bit over-the-top, there was a similar level of comradery between two of the main characters.

The theme of the film was that if you have trouble with a bully, get a bigger bully on your side. I thought about how that was what I saw nightly on the news in international politics. Adults engaged in that behavior, and eventually it was bound to blow our world up. *If adults acted that way, why not teens?* I thought to myself.

I also began to wonder what Jack meant about needing a bodyguard. If he was in danger, or being hurt, I could certainly play the Linderman role to his Clifford. I wasn't certain why that would need to happen, but there was a great deal about which I was uncertain. I knew that Jack fell frequently, and I had seen some bruises. Was it possible that something more was going on?

My thoughts were interrupted during the final fight. Jack jumped out of my lap and was in the aisle cheering and screaming for Linderman and Clifford to "kick their butts!" Dawn tried settling him down, but he was dancing around throwing air punches. The audience was equally engaged and enthused by the dramatic fight.

It was ten o' clock when we exited the theater and began walking back to our neighborhood. Jack was winding down, but he was far from being asleep. Dawn and I walked with him between us holding our hands. We arrived at The Cramer's, about eleven, and Dawn put Jack to bed. He was asleep before I got to his room.

Dawn and I returned to the living room. We stepped outside into the back yard and smoked a bowl of pot before returning to watch some comedy rerun on TV. We fell asleep, and I began having a dream about little animals tap dancing on my back. It was a weird dream, and then I woke up to Jack tickling me and Dawn.

"Hey! The little hand is on the eleven and the big hand is on the six." Jack shook us.

"Oh, damn! You need food, don't you?"

Dawn and I sat up, and Jack started giggling. Dawn had removed her shirt and wasn't wearing a brassiere. I was dressed in a t-shirt and my boxers. Dawn grabbed the blanket and wrapped herself up, grabbed her t-shirt, and retreated to a bathroom. I pulled on my jeans and walked to the kitchen to see what I could make.

I found juice, granola, and rice milk which had to do for the moment. I fixed Jack some breakfast and set him in front of the TV. There was movement upstairs, and I mounted the stairs to hear the sound of running water from the bathroom in the hall. I entered, stripped, and joined Dawn in the shower. We let the water knock the sleep off us and took the opportunity to explore each other while we washed.

Jack was still watching TV when we returned. He looked up at us and smiled.

"I put my dishes on the table in the kitchen. I'm still hungry."

"Want some pizza? Or a cheeseburger? What sounds good?" Dawn sat beside him while I went to wash the dishes and put them away.

I returned a few minutes later, and Dawn was holding Jack in her lap on the couch. "This guy has never had Chinese food before. What do you say we take him to Far Wong's for lunch and then go bowling?"

"Sounds good to me. You ever bowl before, Jack?"

"No. I never have. I don't know how."

I smiled. "I'll show you. It's fun."

We headed out and caught the bus again. Jack was full of energy once more, but Dawn and I were still sort of tired. I let Dawn hold Jack who was looking out the window at everything, and I rested my head against a pole and closed my eyes. Inside of a half hour we arrived outside of Far Wong's traditional Chinese restaurant.

Far Wong didn't serve the kind of overcooked noodle dish that most Chinese American takeout places pass off as Chinese food. The entrees weren't infused with tomato, broccoli, baby corn, and carrot. Instead, there was Bok Choy, Kai-Lan, and water spinach in the food. It made a major difference in quality.

Traditional Chinese cuisine also contains its own regional differences. Much like a southerner would consider northern cornbread to be a cake instead of a bread, the Chinese know what food is from which region. Cantonese food was night and day different from Hunan; a fact that I learned the hard way when I was ten.

Once we were seated, I ordered the Mapo tofu, a dish that was to die for, and three dàbāo. We each had one of these bread-like dumplings filled with bean paste, steamed — which made the buns delightfully squishy and soft — and served with soy sauce. We ordered a pot of Oolong to go with the food. The main dish was spicy, and I watched Jack to make certain he could handle it. He did fine.

After lunch, we headed to the Rock 'n' Bowl Lanes. I paid our entry, and Dawn helped Jack change his shoes. We spent the afternoon teaching Jack how to bowl, and he got to be pretty good for a boy of five. We were on our fourth game when I spotted Max and Glenn from Rabid Flatulence. I turned toward Dawn.

"Hey, should I go ask them about the concert? I mean since they're here and all."

Dawn shrugged. "Sure, why not?"

Jack looked up at me. "A concert? In the park? Can I sing? Is Top Cat going to play? Is Get Lost Jimmy?"

I scooped Jack up and sat him on a counter. I needed to choose my words wisely lest his feelings get hurt. "I'm not sure when the concert will be, but it will be way after your bedtime. Unless your mother goes out of town again, I can't come and take you out late at night. You know? And no, Top Cat said he won't be there. I haven't asked Jimmy yet. Do you even like punk rock music?"

"I don't know. What's punk rock? I like The Wiggles. I like the stuff Top Cat plays."

I scooped Jack up and looked him in the eyes. "Those aren't punk rock. Although I suspect Top Cat probably is more than capable of playing punk. You asked what punk is. I can't readily formalize a definition of punk rock for you, Jack. In its most nascent form, it's non-conformist, and characterized by short formats, fast tempos, distorted riffs, stripped-down instrumentation, and shouted lyrics."

"Oh." He replied.

"Sorry, guy. I can't explain it better than that."

Jack sighed, "I always miss out on the best stuff. Being little isn't fun."

I set him back down on the counter, and Dawn began to tickle him. He laughed and jumped off. I let them bowl a game by themselves while I approached the drummer and lead guitarist from Rabid Flatulence.

"Hello, gentlemen. Nice to see you outside of school."

Max looked over, and his eyes almost bugged out. "Dude, is that Larkspur over there? You and her?"

I spread my hands apart and shrugged. "Weirder things have been known to happen. She's a surprising person."

"Nothing could be weirder than an art fag like you and a cool bitch like her going out, Francis."

"First of all, *Maximillian*, don't call me Francis. Second, don't ever call me a fag. Third, you call her bitch again and you'll get five across the lips."

Max stepped up. "You think you can take me, dude?"

"Take you? Now who's acting homosexual? Who'd want you? I was talking about that five-year-old, anyway. He hears you, and he'll come over here and kill you. He's on probation which is why we're watching him."

"Probation for what" Glenn was incredulous.

"Someone called me Francis, and he shanked them."

The guys laughed, and I laughed with them. "Seriously though, I wanted to ask if your band would be interested in playing at a concert in the park. Dawn and I are getting one together."

Max and Glenn looked at each other, then at me, and then at Dawn. She waved and smiled. Max spoke up. "How did you get a permit for that? I tried at Christmas and was told no."

I threw back my head and laughed. "Did I say anything about a permit? We don't need no stinking permit. We're having a concert. Are you in?"

"Yeah. I have to talk to Jamie, Ryan, and Lester, but yeah, I think we'd be in." Glenn smiled and rubbed his hands together. "I like it."

Max asked, "who else you got?"

"We're asking Sonic Belch, The Kung Fools, Mosh Potatoes, and Dawn is friends with Cricket, Panda, Karma, and Ashley of the Cunning Stunts, so she thinks they can headline. We plan to ask a couple of classical musicians who live in the park to perform, and a jazz group. There's a punk group called Ryan Coke we plan to ask as well."

"Dawn Larkspur hangs out with The Stunners? You got to be

kidding me." Glenn shook his head.

"Like I said, not everything is as it appears."

"Apparently."

The two guys followed me over to Jack and Dawn. I introduced them to Jack, and we all decided to bowl a game together before Dawn and I took Jack home. I managed a 180, and Glenn beat me by twenty points.

After the game Dawn and I took Jack home. It wasn't that late, but he was yawning. Jack went upstairs to put on his pajamas, and I sat with Dawn between my legs massaging her back in front of the TV.

Ten minutes later she was laying on her stomach, her face on a pillow, as I worked out the kinks in her back with the edges of my closed hands. I was straddling her and massaging her when I heard a small growl. I looked up, and Jack was standing there, his hands in fists, looking as if he was having a fit.

"Get your hands off of her! You hit her again, and I'll kill you! I like her. I don't like you anymore. I should have known you were a bad guy. Get away from her!"

I stood up and put my hands up and apart in a sign of calming him down. "I wasn't hitting her, Jack. I was..."

Jack Flash hit me. He hit me ruthlessly and hard. He was short, and I was taller than average, therefore his point of contact hurt. I doubled over, and he kicked me in the shin. The kid was stronger than he looked — and tougher.

I backed away. "Jack, I wasn't hitting her. I was giving her a massage. What did you think I was doing?"

Jack tried attacking me again and Dawn scooped him up still swinging at the air.

"I didn't think nothing. I saw you hitting her, just like the bad guys do to me. You better leave her alone. I don't like you anymore, and I'm telling Mommy to fire you. You're just like Mommy's boyfriend. You're a stupid little nothing. He says that's what I am, but that's what he is!" Jack ranted.

Dawn carried him out of the room. I heard her saying, "dammit, Jack, calm down. He wasn't hurting me, I promise."

As they headed to the kitchen, I began to process what he had just said. The pain from being hit and kicked was replaced by a white-hot rage. Had he just said that someone was beating him up? I recalled the bruises I had seen before. I sat and collected myself. Jack had been acting manic and depressive by turns for two days. Now I figured I knew why. He was hiding something.

Dawn returned holding Jack in her arms. He was calm again. She was crying.

Jack squirmed down and ran toward me. I sidestepped and put my hands up to defend myself. He came over and hugged me hard. "I'm sorry, Cyrus. Please don't hate me. I thought you were hurting her. She said you were just relaxing her back."

"Yeah, I was. Jack, I need to ask you something and you have to level with me. OK?"

Dawn interrupted. "I know what you're going to ask, and the answer is yes. But it's worse than yes."

"Jack, who hurt you? I promise you they won't do it again. I'll end them myself." I held him in my arms.

Dawn shook her head. "Don't do that, Cyrus. Not yet. Jack told me that last week he walked into his mother's bedroom. She was in there with a guy named Carlito. They had bags of what he said looked like sugar. Since she doesn't keep sugar in the kitchen, he asked her what it was. Carlito told him to leave and not ask anything else. Jack kept asking his mother. Carlito took off his belt and beat Jack with it. He had to go to see a doctor, but not at the hospital."

I hugged Jack tighter. This is over, my friend. This is so over. I'll find a way to get you away from that."

Dawn hugged us both. "It gets worse."

"Is that possible?"

"Ms. Cramer took Jack to the post office to get his picture taken for a little blue book."

I set Jack down and swallowed a few times. "A passport? Why?"

"Why do you think? She took off for Mexico and South America. She had something that looked like sugar in bags. Now she's moving out and taking Jack. He doesn't know when."

I sat on the couch and tried to breathe. "We have to do something, but not the cops. Not Top Cat, either. Can't trust him anymore if he won't even get on board with the concert. He's like other adults, I guess. I wouldn't trust our parents. Anyway, my mother said I had to handle any issues that came up. Jimmy might help, but I don't know."

Dawn sat with Jack in her lap and leaned on me. I stared at the TV and tried to figure out what to do. I was in over my head. Jack fell asleep resting on Dawn.

"We have him for two more days and a night. I'll take you both to art class tomorrow. I'll feel out Mr. K. Other than that, we can't do much. I can watch this place on the down-low, and if it looks like they're moving I can find someone to call in something. I don't know."

Dawn gave me a kiss on the cheek. "I just don't want you to try handling this yourself. You'll get killed, or worse. I love you, mister. I am not going to lose you that way."

CHAPTER EIGHTEEN

An hour later we tucked Jack into his bed. I made a search of the master bedroom and the house, but I saw no evidence of drugs. Dawn and I returned to the living room and turned on the TV. *Annie Hall* was on. It was a movie I would otherwise have thoroughly enjoyed. I was too distracted.

I held Dawn close. "After Ms. Cramer comes home, you and I should go find somewhere quiet and get zombie baked. I'm getting sicker of adults with each passing day."

Dawn lay on the couch with her head in my lap. "I know. I lost my mother a long time ago. She's so famous and the world sees this shit-hot perfect woman. She doesn't even understand her own daughter. My father is this rich CFO and to all the world has the perfect life. I can't be like them, but that's what they expect."

"Yeah," I agreed, "my father expects me to be interested in the law and to accept his views about society. Dammit, I'm an artist. I don't want people judging me, and I'm not going to judge them. I wish you and I could take off and go somewhere else. A world where nobody is judging nobody."

"You know," Dawn looked up at me, "My mother would say I'm crazy if she knew how I really am. I'm not crazy and neither

135

are you. We just know bullshit when we see it."

"There's more though," I said. "This thing with Jack, and the conversation we had with Top Cat are driving me crazy mentally. My relationship with you is great but I feel so odd inside. It's something I've never felt before and I don't have words for it. This concert we're planning is going to be great, but what if Top Cat and others are right about it? It's like this afternoon at the amusement park with Jack. We got in that giant teacup and started spinning 'round and 'round and 'round. My life feels like that every day now. Like I'm spinning 'round and 'round and the ride won't stop."

Dawn held me and we sat watching the movie. We finally fell asleep, and when we woke up, Jack was sitting on me changing the channels.

"Hey, Jack. I'm not a chair. Sit on the couch, please." I got erect and had a good stretch.

Dawn woke up and stood. I let her use the guest bathroom first, and then I took my turn in the shower. We joined Jack again in the living room and watched the end of a cartoon.

"You guys hungry?" Dawn asked. "I could go for some donuts and coffee, or something."

Jack jumped to his feet, "yes. I'm very hungry. Can we go to the park, too?"

I stood and turned off the TV. We all headed outside and walked a few blocks to a corner store. I bought Jack a chocolate milk, and a coffee each for me and Dawn. She bought a dozen Boston cream donuts pre-boxed. With our breakfast purchased we headed to the park.

When we arrived, I saw Top Cat playing guitar. Instead of going over I directed Dawn and Jack toward the playground. I wasn't sure about Top Cat after he tried to dissuade me and

Dawn from our concert plans, and after what I knew about Jack being abused, I wasn't certain which adults I could trust. I hoped that Top Cat wouldn't notice us. In that, my luck was not to be.

"Hey dudes," Top Cat approached us, "I haven't seen you in a couple of days. How are things?"

Dawn scowled, "get lost! We don't need adults around."

"What's with that noise? You have a problem?" Top Cat was terse. "I thought we were friends. If there's an issue let's talk about it. Maybe I can help."

I stood and got face to face with the man. "Maybe you can't. We'll handle our own problems, got it? Just leave us alone."

Top Cat had a look of genuine concern on his face, and when I looked at Jack he was starting to cry. "Leave, man. You're scaring my buddy here."

Top Cat turned and left. He continued down the path and out of sight. I scooped up Jack and held him.

"Sorry, Jack. I don't really feel like having adults around right now. I don't know who the bad guys are and who the good guys are anymore. It's nothing you did."

Jack wiped his eyes and nose on his sleeve. "I thought Top Cat was a good guy."

Dawn hugged us both. "I used to think so. Now – I just don't know anymore. He sounds like he's on our side, and we do have to tell someone what's going on. On the other hand, he also acts like every other adult who tries to stop me from taking action to fix the world."

"He helped us get the park people bratwursts," Jack said.

I nodded. "He did do that. He also tried to tell me and Dawn not to hold our concert. I don't know what he'd do if I told him someone was hurting you. He might help, but he might not."

Jack panicked. "You can't tell anyone I told you. I wasn't supposed to tell. Please don't tell anyone."

Dawn scooped him up and calmed him. He stopped crying and rested his head on her shoulder. The three of us finished our breakfast and walked along the garden path. We were making the turn on the far side when we spotted Get Lost Jimmy and Swee'pea on a bench. I wasn't sure if he was any better than other adults, but I didn't have time to decide. Jack ran over and started petting the dog.

"Hi, Jimmy." Dawn and I both said.

"Hello. How are things?"

Dawn sat on one side of Jimmy and I on the other. Dawn sighed, "Things are complicated. I can't say much, but they aren't so good right now."

Jimmy gave us a look of palpable concern. "Anything I can do to help?"

"I don't know." I replied. "I have been meaning to ask you something, though. Dawn and I are planning a concert in the park in maybe a week or two. Would you like to play? Top Cat said he won't and gave us some jive reason why we shouldn't do it."

Jimmy cleared his throat. "Swee'pea and I have to return home in the next few days. I have to get back to my career. I wish I could stay for your concert, but my vacation is ending."

Jack jumped up and wrapped his arms around Jimmy's considerable frame. "I'll miss seeing you and Swee'pea."

Jimmy returned the hug. "I'll miss you, too. I might return next summer. I haven't decided just yet."

Dawn started to speak, stopped, and started again. "May I ask you a hypothetical question?"

"You may." Jimmy smiled at her.

"Let's say you had a friend. Let's say you found out that someone was hurting that friend, and you couldn't call the police or handle it yourself. What would you do?"

Jimmy stroked his beard and pondered. "Depending on the age of the friend, I would most likely tell someone I trusted about the situation. Sometimes a problem shared is a problem halved."

Dawn looked at Jack, and then at me, and then back at Jimmy. "That's the problem. We don't know who to trust."

"That is a problem. I would like to think I could help, but we are acquaintances more than friends. I do see why you're having a conflict. Between this hypothetical friend, and this concert you have planned, that's a lot on your plate."

"Yes, it is." I agreed. "I'm glad we had a chance to meet you and hear you play, man. You're pretty cool for an adult."

Jimmy chuckled, and then grew serious. "Just know this, Cyrus, Dawn; you have something supremely special inside of you. Both of you. There's a seed that contains your unique self. With this concert, and other matters, you may feel like you're standing all alone, and that's a pretty scary place to be. I know about that place. Don't ask me how, but I do. Things may transpire where you find that you have to trust someone, anyone. It will feel like jumping off a tall building into the darkness. How desperate that feels, those moments before you jump. When the time comes, you just got to do it. You have to find that inner-strength and you must jump."

Dawn and I nodded and hugged Jimmy one last time. He was a good man, and I was sorry to see him leave.

"I'm going to miss hearing you blowing your harps, man." I smiled.

Dawn planted a kiss on his hirsute cheek. "Take care of your son, there. I wish you both the best."

Jimmy had a tear in his eye. "I know that there are people discouraging your plans. Personally, I admire you both for taking a stand. It might not work out this time, or the next. You are willing to try. Yes, I admire that. The world is ripe. The people in this park are ripe. It's time our nation got in touch with that place inside that craves solidarity more than division; honesty more than etiquette: life more than soundbites."

Dawn, Jack, and I gave Jimmy another hug and continued walking. I was the last time I saw or heard from the man. I thought about his words often for the next ten days. He had something to tell us, and he turned out to be correct.

CHAPTER NINETEEN

awn and I took Jack home. We had one more day together. Ms. Cramer would be home the next afternoon, and I still was uncertain how to deal with her. I had no notion of calling the police. I wanted to tell someone, but there was no one I trusted anymore except Dawn. Handling it myself was what I had in mind, but I knew that Dawn objected to this possibility.

Once home, Dawn and I settled onto the couch with Jack between us. Dawn smiled at him.

"You asked before what punk rock music is. You want to hear some, Jack?"

Jack jumped up. "Yes, please. Do you have any tapes or records?"

Dawn nodded, "I have a tape of Eight Ball. I also have some CDs of The Ramones, Stray Cats, and Operation Ivy, and Misfits."

I stood and turned on the stereo. "There are local bands, too, but the ones Dawn mentioned are up there in national recognition."

Dawn put in her tape of Eight Ball, and soon Jack was grooving to "Young and Insane." She and I danced, and Jack joined in. It helped me to put aside my thoughts about more serious issues.

I had time to figure everything out, and I would.

We spent the rest of the day listening to music, watching TV, and eating pizza and pop. That evening I had an art class, and I took Jack and Dawn with me.

"Hey, Jack. When I'm not hanging out with you, I take art classes. You want to come see it?"

Jack nodded. "Can I draw too? Like we do sometimes in the park?"

"I think that would be OK. My teacher will probably like the stuff you draw. I know I do."

Dawn smiled. "You're a really good artist. Both of you are."

We helped Jack get cleaned up, and changed his shirt which had some pizza stains on it. I gave Jack a piggyback ride as we walked to the college where I took my summer art class. Dawn and Jack stood behind me as I approached Mr. K. "Can I speak with you after class? I need some advice."

"Certainly, Cyrus. I'm honored that you would ask my help. You look worried, is it something that can wait until later?"

"It can wait until after class. By the way, you know Dawn Larkspur from school. This young man is Jack Flash. I babysit for him, and tonight his mother is out of town. We aren't doing anything that would be inappropriate if he sat in, are we?"

Mr. K chuckled. "We never do. I know that you want to move up to the class with the nude models, Cyrus, but that's going to have to wait until you are actually in college. I don't feel comfortable allowing a fifteen-year-old into those."

As it turned out we did have a model that night. Dawn sat beside me with Jack and watched as I painted the lady who had been invited that night. She was dressed in tight jeans and a pink blouse with rhinestone encrusted cowboy boots and a matching hat. I focused on not only capturing her, but the room details around her. It wasn't my best work, but I thought it was decent. It would work for a college portfolio. Jack had attempted to sketch her in pencil on a piece of paper I gave him. He did well enough for his age.

After class, Mr. K. approached me, Dawn, and Jack. "You doing OK, Cyrus? Miss Larkspur I thank you for joining us. I didn't realize that you had an interest in art."

"I'm thinking about taking a beginner class next term. I'm not as good at it as Cyrus, but I do draw some. I mostly draw designs and abstract stuff." Dawn blushed.

"That's fine. If it comes from inside of you then it is good art. I'll enjoy seeing some of your work."

Jack handed Mr. K his sketch. "I tried to draw that girl, too. I don't know if it's a very good drawing."

Mr. K looked at the sketch with a critical eye. "This is fine work for a beginner. You're what? Six? Seven?"

"I'm five." Jack smiled.

"Then this is quite well done. Keep practicing. The more you practice the better you will become." Mr. K turned to me. "Now then, Cyrus?"

I sighed, tried to start, and then paused. I swallowed hard and tried again. "Let's say that hypothetically a friend of mine had a neighbor who was young. Let's say that my friend found out that the neighbor was being hurt. Let's say that the parents might be involved in drug trafficking. How do I advise my friend to proceed?"

Mr. K lowered himself into a chair. "That's a lot of hypotheticals. If you know that someone is abusing someone and might be involved with drugs, the idea of calling the police isn't a bad one. It can be done anonymously from a pay phone."

"My friend doesn't trust the cops. My friend doesn't really

trust many adults."

"You're not the friend, right Dawn?" Mr. K looked concerned.

"I can honestly say I'm not." She looked back and forth at us.

Mr. K looked down at Jack and then shook his head slightly. "I won't ask that." He said to himself. "My only advice is that you need to tell someone in authority. The police are the best people to inform. The sooner you do that, the sooner the situation is handled."

"Thank you. I'll let my friend know what you suggested." I said and stood.

Dawn and I took turns carrying Jack on the way home.

He was exhausted and fell asleep with his head on our shoulders. After Jack was tucked into bed, Dawn and I tidied the house, and she took all evidence of junk food and carried it down the block to someone else's trash cans.

The next morning, we went out for breakfast at a bakery, returned to Jack's house, and watched TV until the middle of the afternoon. Ms. Cramer returned. Jack was up in his room, dressed in slacks and a polo shirt, looking at picture books. It was everything I could do not to attack Ms. Cramer and tell her what I thought of her and her boyfriend. Dawn had already left to return home. Ms. Cramer set her suitcases next to the door and looked at me.

"Cyrus, I have some news and I need to discuss it with you."

I took a seat. "Yes? Is there a problem?" I tried to sound nonchalant.

"Not a problem, no. I have been offered a position south of the border. I'll be placing this house on the market, but Jeremiah and I will be moving in a couple of weeks. That being said, your services will not be needed going forward. I realize that this is an inconvenience as I had promised you employment for the summer. I am prepared to pay you one thousand dollars as compensation. However, I must ask you something in return."

My eyes widened, and my jaw went slack. A grand was more than enough to cover my art supplies and other educational needs for most of the rest of my school career. "What would that be?"

"My job involves the potential for corporate espionage and internal struggles. If anyone were to ask if you know me, or were to ask anything about me, I would like you to demur. Our business is no one else's."

I nodded and thought to myself, "*no worries, bitch. I won't tell anyone what's going on. I want the pleasure of breaking your neck myself.*"

Ms. Cramer wrote me a check and started upstairs. I left and walked home. Once there, I telephoned Dawn.

"I can't believe it. First, she acts like nothing is going on out of the ordinary, and then she pays me a thousand bucks to keep my mouth shut. I need to put this check into my savings account, but then maybe we can hit the movies. Just the two of us. I need to hang out and let everything go for a while. I think you probably do as well."

Dawn yawned. "The movies would be fun. Maybe we can hook up with The Cunning Stunts there. I'll call and ask. I need a nap for a few hours first. I'm really worn out. What time is the movie?"

"They're showing *Grease* and *West Side Story* starting at six. You take a nap. Dream about me. I'll clean up and get this money deposited. I can come get you at five."

We hung up and I went to take a shower. I needed to figure out how to handle all the problems life was throwing at me. I also needed to destress and forget about anything except having fun. These were contradictory needs as far as I could determine. I was fifteen and I felt as if I was treading water way beyond my depth. I needed Dawn around as much as possible so that I wouldn't come unglued. As I stood under the pulsating stream of the shower the stress finally took its toll. I began to sob uncontrollably.

CHAPTER TWENTY

Grease was a blast and just the sort of release that Dawn and I needed. From the opening credits, the audience was animated and singing along with the soundtrack. Dawn and I joined in. We also spent time making out and feeling each other up in the balcony. The members of The Cunning Stunts had shown up and Dawn introduced me. They sat one row in front of us and recited the Pink Ladies' lines from memory in synch with the movie. It was a fun evening.

West Side Story was as great a musical as I recalled. Neither Dawn nor I had seen the stage version, but the movie packed a great deal of power into every scene. The audience didn't do a sing along with *West Side Story*, but there were a few people around us crying by the end. Even members of The Cunning Stunts were in tears.

Dawn and I invited the ladies to get sandwiches and sodas. They agreed and while we ate, we discussed the upcoming concert and the movies we had just seen. It felt wonderful to be in the company of my peers, and it took the edge off of my emotions.

I swallowed a bite of my pastrami on rye and dabbed spicy brown mustard from my mouth with a napkin.

"The pairing of those movies is interesting," I said. "*Grease*, wherever Rydell is supposed to be, shows gangs as almost light-hearted groups of outsiders who want to be outsiders. Even The Scorpions come across as less than the hardest kids on the block. The T-Birds and Pink Ladies are lovers, not fighters. They put on an act, but they're inherently goofy in their way."

Dawn nodded. "I agree. *West Side Story* was written closer to the timeframe it's showing. The gangs are embittered and vicious. I mean Baby-John is kind of a weak link, but the other Jets or Sharks would clean the floor with Kenickie. I'd love to see Crater-Face Balmudo in a fight with Action or Tony. He'd get his ass handed back to him."

Cricket swallowed a bite of food, brushed her aqua high-lighted hair from her eyes, and nodded in agreement. "Yeah. It's almost like one was written more for the disco era and the other was showing the reality that was gang life. Furthermore, *West Side Story*, is a retelling of *Romeo and Juliet.* I read that in English class before I dropped out. I'm not sure if Warren Casey based *Grease* on his life or not."

I thought about that. "I see your point. They're both well-constructed stories. The love affair between Tony and Maria could be seen as similar to the love between Danny and Sandy. I admit that I don't know much about real gang life except from the movies and some reading I've done."

Panda laughed. "It's no surprise that you don't know much about gangs. You and Dawn are uptown. I mean, she hangs out with us and come around from time to time in the park, but she's still upper tier. I'm not criticizing. I just call things like they are, man."

"I enjoy the music, but you're right. That's why I want to hold this concert. I want to become more familiar with those who live a more normal life. I want to give something back."

Ashley and Karma shook their heads. "There is nothing normal about the lives of people who are unhoused. You're basically slumming is what you're doing." Karma looked irritated.

"Hey," Ashley chimed in, "he's trying to arrange a concert. He was part of a protest to help change things in the park where that one vendor is concerned. Change has to start somewhere. Let's not be too critical."

I finished my food. "I'm sorry if you see it as I'm slumming, or Dawn is. I didn't ask to be born an upper-middle-class white male. I do everything I can to not behave like the people with whom I am expected to associate."

Dawn put up her hands in a sign of truce and ending arguments. "He's right. He does everything he can. You're right that he and I aren't anything but middle-class pretenders to the scene. So, let's quit being defensive. I thought we were here to enjoy ourselves."

"Back to the movies, if you want to see some real gangs, check out *The Warriors*. Now that's a gang movie." Karma smiled.

"One of my favorites," I replied. "I took this kid I know named Jack to see that before Dawn and I hooked up, but he fell asleep during it."

"You did what?" Dawn gave me a look. "You took a five-year-old to see that? Cyrus, that's seriously not a cool move. You could have traumatized him."

"I know. I've already kicked my own butt about it. Plus, it was an all-night movie triple feature. *Over The Edge* and *Times Square* were also playing. If I could have a do-over I wouldn't do that again."

Dawn laughed. "So, in a three-way fight between Jets, T-Birds, and Warriors, who would win?"

"Warriors all the way. Although, Baby-John and Cowboy might be a fair match-up." Cricket laughed and the other three members of The Cunning Stunts nodded in agreement.

"Or Rembrandt." I chimed in

"Him too." Ashley agreed. "Snowball or Cochise, though? They'd wipe the floor with The Jets, The Sharks, and every T-Bird. Swan and Ajax would, too. The T-Birds are on the level of The Orphans. I might put The Jets or The Sharks up with The Baseball Furies or The Turnbulls."

I paid the bill. Dawn and I said our farewells and our group exited. Dawn and I walked one direction while the other ladies walked toward the park.

"Are you feeling any better, Cyrus?" Dawn held my hand.

"Not really. I can't figure a way to help Jack. I want to go over there and start busting heads, but I promise I won't. Not yet. When the time comes, I'll make my move."

I walked Dawn to her house. We kissed, and I watched her go inside. I was tired. My heart was beating faster. I felt sweat forming inside of my shirt despite the night being a bit cooler than normal. Once inside my house I took a shower and walked downstairs to the kitchen. Mrs. Ferrigno was mixing batter for a chocolate layer cake. I poured myself a glass of milk.

"Hey, Mrs. F? I know you've read *Romeo and Juliet*. Have you ever seen *West Side Story* performed on stage?"

"I have. I saw both a few times both on Broadway and in local productions. Both are grand stories."

"I saw the movie of *West Side Story* this evening. I was talking to my girlfriend, Dawn, about it. We read *Romeo and Juliet* last year in English class.

"There are similarities and differences, but both pieces can speak to kids from any era." Mrs. Ferrigno said. "I mean look at just the idea of friendship. Although less so as we age, in youth the friends one makes factor greatly into a kid's decision-making process and actions. It is human nature to be affected by the thoughts and opinions of those we consider our friends. Tony wasn't going to be at the dance, but his best friend Riff persuaded him to attend. That set off the romance which ended in tragedy. Romeo had his own situations with Mercutio."

"Yeah, I can see that. I try not to be influenced by my friends, but Dawn used to be a lot. She's changed this summer." I carefully avoided the fact that Dawn had friends amongst the homeless and the punk rockers.

"Exactly. Then there's the trope of the star-crossed lovers. This was a literary device in 1553 and in 1953 and still is used in 1993." Mrs. Ferrigno stirred her batter. "Even with the love situations, friendship had an effect. Despite fulfilling twin roles, the Nurse and Anita provided very distinct impacts to Juliet and Maria as the courses of their respective stories unfolded. The lives of both pairs of lovers ultimately ended in tragedy, but they were affected along the way by distinctly diverse friends. Their friends had abundant influence in their actions."

I finished my milk. "I get that. I guess even in this day and age we need to watch how much our friends effect our behavior."

"You certainly do, Francis."

I walked upstairs to my room and put on my earphones. I cranked up a tape of The Dead Kennedy's and listened as I thought about my relationship with Dawn. Once we returned to school, we'd both face a great deal of antagonism and hassle about our being a couple. Dawn's former crowd didn't like me much because I refused to act like I was better than others due to my financial status. My crowd, if I had one, was generally looked down upon by the other cliques because they were outcasts and artists. It wouldn't be easy, but Mrs. Ferrigno was correct. Dawn and I had to make our stand despite what our friends had to say. Those friends at school anyway. I began to consider the other friends we had made. Dawn was friends with kids in the park. I was friendly with Hetty and other homeless denizens. I had gotten to know Get Lost Jimmy, but was that truly a friendship? Top Cat was a question mark. Uncle Don had disappeared off of the radar. Neither of them was a friend in the ordinary sense. Jack was a friend, albeit much younger.

I turned off the tape player and went to bed. I needed to sort out varying and conflicting issues in my head. Sleep helped bring clarity most of the time. If it failed to do so I could at least delay my decisions until a later time.

CHAPTER TWENTY-ONE

For the next week Dawn and I worked on the plans for our concert. We met with the members of various bands, and we met with some of the homeless in the park who played instruments. We decided to start in the evening with some jazz, and a bit of classical music. That way we might lure any cops into a sense of well-being about our concert. We would start the punk rock portion after it was properly dark out.

Dawn said that she knew people who could access amplifiers and a few spotlights. I was in charge of creating and printing the flyers. In the midst of our plans, we spotted Uncle Don one afternoon in the park. He was sitting chatting with Top Cat.

"Uncle Don. Long time no see" I offered him my hand and deliberately ignored the presence of Top Cat.

Uncle Don smiled at me and Dawn. "Hello my young friends. Where is your ward? You used to have a young boy with you."

I nodded. "The job ended. His mother said that she's moving out of the country. Something related to her work. I wish they weren't, but she says they must."

"I see. Well, that's interesting. You're out of work, and I'm resuming work. My station negotiated a contract. I have returned to close up my summer home and then I shall return to my main domicile. It's been nice getting to know you, Cyrus.

Dawn. One day you'll hear from me again. I assure you that our paths will again cross."

Dawn and I shook his hand and started walking away. Top Cat approached from behind us. "Hold up, you both. I need to talk to you."

"What?" I scowled.

"I don't know what happened, or maybe I do. You were friendly with me until I suggested that your concert isn't a good idea. Suddenly I've become your enemy. That isn't how I want to leave things, dudes. I know that you're doing what you feel you have to do. I was your age once, believe it or not. I made my stands as well. I can't agree with your plans, but don't get the idea that I reject your desire to see them out. You're both young. You don't understand everything yet."

Dawn shrugged. "OK. You aren't for us, but you aren't against us either. We get that. I'm sorry if you think we're being rude, but you also don't understand everything. We have bigger problems than you not agreeing with a concert. We have a friend who is in big trouble, and we have to handle that. The concert is another matter. You don't want to be involved, then don't be."

Top Cat nodded. "I understand. I hope things work out for your friend. I'm heading out of town for a few weeks. I have some things that I need to attend to, dudes. If I don't see you again, I wanted to leave things better than us being enemies."

I reluctantly put out my hand. "It was nice knowing you. I apologize if I hurt your feelings, but this summer went south in a hurry. If we see you again, we'll say hello. You play a mean guitar, Top Cat."

Top Cat gave us a thumbs up. "Life has a way of doing that very thing, dudes; falling apart at the most inopportune times."

Dawn and I walked away, and Top Cat returned to Uncle Don. I was ready for the concert, and I was worried about Jack. My stomach felt sour, but at the same time excitement coursed through my veins. I needed an outlet, but with my parents at home, and Mrs. Ferrigno, and with Dawn's mother and father at home, the obvious outlet for my manic energy wasn't available. I didn't think that making the beast in the woods was a great idea on the spur of the moment.

"How about we hit the fitness club?" I asked.

"Sounds good to me," Dawn replied. "We have to go back to your house and mine to get our workout clothes, but yeah, that sounds good."

We walked back to our respective domiciles and collected the necessary clothing. I grabbed my bike and the locks for it and walked it to Dawn's. She emerged fifteen minutes later with her bike. We rode to the fitness club, and I signed us in. The workout was exactly what I needed.

We had finished with the treadmills and weights, and I was standing in front of a heavy bag. No one else was in the room except me and Dawn. I pictured Ms. Cramer standing in front of me, and Jack standing by the wall. Executing a roundhouse kick, I made the bag swing and the chain rattle.

"Careful there, Cyrus. You'll tear that thing out of the ceiling." Dawn gasped.

"It's better than tearing apart Ms. Cramer and that bastard boyfriend of hers."

Dawn approached and wrapped her arms around me. "I know you can't let it go. I can't either. But we have to. We can't fix that problem. Not unless we let the cops in, or we let someone else with authority in. I don't want to ask my mother. She knows all the words to say on the radio, but I'm not so sure she would help out. My Father definitely wouldn't. He thinks there's nothing wrong with taking a belt to a kid."

I kissed Dawn full on the mouth. We held that for a few minutes, and then stopped for air. "He doesn't still hit you, does he?"

She blushed. "Sometimes. If he gets really pissed off, he will. It doesn't happen like it did a few years ago."

I stepped to one side, pictured Mr. Larkspur in front of me, and punched the heavy bag with a salvo that rocked it back and forth. "That's what I think about anyone taking a strap to you."

Dawn smiled at me, "well my father and mother shouldn't anyway." She giggled and blushed more.

I shook my head. "You're crazy, girl."

"Crazy in love with you, yes I am."

We walked to the steam room and sat for a while holding each other. My body began to relax, and my emotions returned to a more normal setting. I lifted Dawn in my arms and carried her to the hot tub. We held each other and sat necking for a half hour.

After entering our respective changing rooms and showering, we met in the lobby. I didn't feel like heading home, and I couldn't think of anything to kill the time.

"You want to head to the mall and hang out? Go back to the park? What? I don't feel like sitting in my room being bored."

Dawn nodded in agreement. "It's strange not having the kid around. I guess we could head to the mall. I don't want to lock our bikes outside there, though. We could park our bikes at our houses and I could grab my pipe and stuff. We could go get baked and walk around the mall. We could sit in the park, too. I think we have everything squared away for the concert, so that isn't really needing our attention."

Somehow the afternoon got killed as did the following day and the day after that. I hadn't realized how dull life was without work. I couldn't imagine life apart from Dawn anymore. Something inside of me was changing and I didn't have words to describe it.

The third afternoon I did five sketches of Dawn at various locations. That night I showed four of them to Mr. K. I would have shown him the fifth, but it was done from memory, and Dawn was unclothed in it.

Mr. K looked over my sketches. "You're getting there, Cyrus. You are almost as good as some of my adult students. I still prefer your abstracts and your still life sketches of nature. Given time you will improve at drawing human forms. It might be the hardest area to master."

Dawn watched me as I painted a bowl of fruit on a pedestal. I watched her sketch the same subject in colored pencil. She had a certain Picasso influence in her work. Mr. K noticed that as well. He agreed to let her attend for the rest of the summer, but he couldn't allow her the college credits.

The days passed and then it was showtime. The concert was finally going to happen, and it was about time. The tension in my chest and head had reached a climax. I was ready to break the chain and run with the wolves as some philosopher or another once wrote.

CHAPTER TWENTY-TWO

Dawn and I ate dinner at Far Wong's and walked through some art studios in the surrounding area before heading to the park. The professional artists put my work to shame, but it was inspiring to see that a future existed if I worked for it. Dawn and I stopped every now and then to hug, kiss, and just hold hands. I was full of nervous tension, and the excitement radiating from Dawn was palpable.

We arrived at the park and there everyone was. A number of old ladies stood in a cluster holding tambourines, maracas, and assorted handheld percussion instruments. Men were tuning up brass and woodwind instruments. The members of Sonic Belch had brought speakers, as had Ashley and Karma from The Cunning Stunts. They set everything up on a stage where the spring flower shows took place.

The flowers in the garden were blooming so bright under the full moon that I felt a warmth deep inside my soul. Members of the Rabid Flatulence were walking here and there chatting with people and tuning their instruments. They began warming up with the members of Ryan Coke. I wasn't certain the Kung Fools would make the show, but they appeared at the last minute and began warming up. The Mosh Potatoes stayed on the sidelines.

A half hour later a classical group took to the stage. Two

cellos, three violins, a viola, and a man with a standing bass began to play soft melodies. I stood in the back with Dawn, and we smoked a bowl of pot. Although classical music had never been my favorite, the sound was exceptional under the influence of strong buds.

The group played for a half hour, and then a jazz quintet took over. The music they played was meant for dancing, and many of the older people began to swing and jitterbug. Dawn and I slipped away into the darkness and smoked some more. I was on edge and waiting for the punk rock portion of the concert to take over. I held Dawn in my arms, and suddenly we were on the ground. I managed to put on protection before we went at it, but the session was desperately needed by both of us.

Dawn and I dusted ourselves off, cleaned up as best we could, and returned to the concert. Cricket, of The Cunning Stunts, approached. "Where did you two get off to? There's a huge crowd forming now, and I think we better get this concert into high gear before they get testy."

We walked through the crowds, and sure enough the population of homeless had tripled in size. People were playing whatever instruments they had, harmonizing out of key, lacking in pitch but enjoying themselves. It was a sight to behold, and I felt as if we had already made a difference just by holding this much of a concert.

On the outer edges I noticed that two groups of skinheads had shown up. There were also a number of other teens with mohawks, and other non-traditional hairstyles. The angst was palpable. Dawn and I moved toward the front, and she took the microphone.

"OK, folks. This is it. Time to rock out with your...you know the rest."

The crowd roared their approval at her opening.

"I'm glad everyone could make it, but please keep things cool. No fighting. No violence. This is about showing the city leaders that we can do this without brawls and bullshit. So, without further ado, I give you The Mosh Potatoes."

The band took the stage, and they weren't good. I mean they had almost no musical skills. I had never heard them play, nor had Dawn. They might have been friends with The Kung Fools, but they were not the opening band I would have chosen otherwise. The singers six-inch-tall, rainbow dyed, spike-mohawk, and the bassists ten-gallon afro were an interesting sight, but the group lacked any sort of a message. They screamed obscenities to no purpose and the singer was off key. I let them play three songs, and then motioned them to exit the stage.

Rabid Flatulence followed the Potatoes, and they redeemed the mood. They were all teens who attended Valley of Hinnom Institute with me and Dawn. As they played, teens began to pogo and headbang. Soon a mosh pit was formed, and the wild frenzy of swinging feet and fists began. Dawn and I watched, but we didn't join in. Many of the older people began to move back toward the outer edges of the concert.

After Rabid Flatulence was The Kung Fools. They were alright, but they needed more cohesion. They were more of a high school garage band, each doing their own thing, than they were anything like a professional group. However, they were also entertaining. They were followed by Sonic Belch who were also not terrible. I enjoyed their sound, and their message, but they weren't the best. I understood why Dawn found them sophomoric, but I felt that if they had some management there was a future for them.

Once Sonic Belch took over, the show again took shape. They were a mixed race, mixed ethnicity band. As much punk rock as they were a rockabilly swing band, they had the makings of something influential if they stuck together.

Their lead singer, Cholito, struck a pose on the stage like Elvis Presley. He kicked out one foot and began a rimshot routine. "Are you ready to Rock and Roll!?"

"Yeah!" The crowd roared back at him.

"I can't hear you!"

"Yeah!" The crowd screamed.

"Alright then! But, first, I need to address something. Dawn stated at the beginning that this concert has to show the authorities that we can do this without committing crimes. I've already seen some of you starting fights and instigating nonsense. For a long time, this park hasn't allowed concerts. We don't got permits for this one, either. We're doing this for you, the people who live here in this park. You, and every citizen of this damned nation who are being oppressed is being stood up for tonight. We are here to have a good time. We are here to play our music and dance. I got nothing against mosh pits, but if the authorities see people trying to hit and kick each other, even in the name of dancing, they will shut us down. So be cool, and have a ball, that's what it's all about after all."

Sonic Belch began playing their opening number, "Strutting on Main Street." As they played, two groups of skinheads began moving through the crowd toward the stage. I sensed something amiss and grabbed Dawn by the hand.

"We need to get to the back, now. I think there's about to be a fight." I screamed over the crowd.

Dawn pulled away from me and ran to the stage. Sonic Belch finished their set and exited the stage. Ryan Coke began to play, and the mood settled a bit. The band was in the middle of a cover of Twisted Sister when all Hell broke loose.

One group of skinheads, adorned in American flag patches and military style clothing faced off with a group of skinheads who had swastika tattoos and wore brown shirts and jackboots. What started as a dance-off between two members on each side grew ugly fast. Out came knives, chains, broken bottles, and brass knuckles. I grabbed Dawn once more and took off running. Homeless people scattered, and pandemonium ensued.

As Dawn and I ran from the crowds, I noticed that police cars had surrounded the area. There were flashers and spinners, and a loud voice boomed over a speaker system attached to a police van.

"Everyone is commanded to disperse, now! If you do not disperse you will be arrested. You are in violation of city ordinance 21.9911. Disperse now!" The voice boomed.

Before we could find an exit, a cop grabbed me and Dawn by the arms. We were hustled over to a bench and forced to sit. The cop scowled at us and radioed someone.

Looking down at me, another overweight police officer demanded, "What's your name, boy?"

"Cyrus Ahriman." I told him.

"Young lady?"

"Dawn Larkspur."

"Your mother is the lady from the radio, right?"

Dawn glared. "I have nothing more to say. I want a lawyer, now."

The cop reached for his club, "we can do this the easy way or the hard way. Your choice."

I started to stand, and he shoved me back down. "You pull that club on us, and I'll shove it up your ass. You have nothing on us. We were dispersing like you told us."

A third officer approached and dismissed the other two. "Well, if it isn't the bratwurst kid and his lady companion. I'm Chief White. What's going on here? You're both in a mess of trouble, you know that, right?"

Dawn looked scared for once. She started to cry. I reached over and held her close. "Look, Chief, take us downtown and I'll explain everything. Just keep your stormtroopers at bay. We aren't out to hurt anyone, and neither are most of these people."

As we followed behind Chief White, Dawn cuffed to me by a wrist, I saw a large number of homeless denizens laying on the ground beaten and bloody. The poor souls who had come alive this summer, for whom Dawn and I had created the concert, were again destroyed. I sensed that everything we had done had been for naught. All the skinheads were in handcuffs, and there were vans being loaded with people of all ages.

Reporters had converged on the scene, cameras flashing, people yelling questions. One reporter shoved a camera toward me and Dawn. We used out free hands to give him the finger. A blonde TV reporter with enormous breasts tried to block the progress of Chief White and us in order to ask me and Dawn questions. I shouted a few obscenities at her. Chief White ordered her to step aside, and he put us into the back of his car.

CHAPTER TWENTY-THREE

D awn and I were driven to the police station and ushered into an office. Dawn was pale and had a look in her eyes like a deer in the headlights. My stomach was cramped, and I was beginning to wish that I had never thought about holding the concert.

Chief White motioned to a desk cop. "Hey, see if you can get these two some Cokes." He looked at both of us in turn. "Now then, how about you both tell me what happened back there in the park? Cyrus, what was all that violence you instigated?"

My mouth came open and I closed it. I swallowed and tried to speak. "Instigated? I instigated nothing. We were attempting to hold a concert for the people in the park. Those idiots who were fighting weren't with us and we don't know them."

Dawn sighed and began crying again. "Look, we were just trying to do some good for people who have it bad. Can't you let us go? We won't do it again."

Chief White shook his head. Our Cokes arrived and Dawn and I began drinking. Chief White smiled pleasantly. "I appreciate that you want to help people. I do. I appreciate that you were able to get the vendors to sell bratwurst again. I enjoy them for lunch. The problem we have here is that there is a reason we can't allow concerts in the park. You might understand that better now."

I nodded. "We understand that. Our problem is that you are lumping everyone in the park together. If we were allowed to have the concerts, and if you cops would maybe watch the area, then we could do something good, and you could keep out the troublemakers."

Chief White held out his hands to the side, palms up. "If you can find a way to get the taxpayers to support that come and find me. I don't work for free and neither does anyone here. We are supported by tax dollars. Not yours yet. Your parents, though, they pay taxes to finance the police department. They are the ones who tell the city council how to operate by voting people in and out. This isn't as simple as some loudmouth teenagers wanting to fix the ills of society."

I said nothing. Dawn didn't speak. The air in the room was all of a sudden thick and heavy. Chief White broke the silence. "We have to call your parents and hers. I'm glad you didn't try bringing you little brother to this situation. I'll give you credit for having that much sense."

Dawn started crying again, sobbing would be a better word for it. "He isn't Cyrus' brother or mine. He's in a lot of trouble anyway."

I glared at Dawn, but she ignored me. "You could help with that. I don't know if you will."

Chief White looked interested, "tell me more about that situation while we wait for your parents. If I can help you I will."

I shook my head. "I doubt it. I doubt any adult will ever help us. I appreciate that you're playing good cop here, and I don't much want to see the bad cops, but I know the truth. You are supported by the taxpayers and adults who run society. That puts you squarely in opposition to our causes."

Chief White gave me a stern look. "You're a real hard ass, aren't you? Just sit there and keep your mouth shut. Let this young lady tell me what it is she has to say."

Dawn dried her eyes and wiped her nose on her sleeve. "Cyrus has been babysitting for that kid all summer. Once he and I hooked up I started helping him. We became friends with him, sort of, and even babysat a few times overnight. His mother goes away on business for days at a time and pays Cyrus really well to watch the kid. She's moving though, and so we don't babysit anymore."

Chief White cleared his throat. "So, what's the issue? What's the trouble?"

I thought for a moment and figured that we couldn't be in any more trouble than we were. "The problem is that when I first started babysitting, I noticed that Jack was skittish. His real name is Jeremiah Carlson Cramer. I call him Jack because he likes it. The first time I babysat overnight I was helping him get ready for his bath and I noticed some ugly bruising on his butt, back, and legs. I asked about the bruises, and he said he fell down and hurt himself. I didn't think anything more about it. That might have been stupid on my part,"

Dawn took a sip of Coke. "When Cyrus and I were babysitting for a few days another time, we were messing around after he went to bed. Cyrus was giving me a massage and Jack came downstairs and saw us. He attacked Cyrus because he thought Cyrus was hurting me. I took him to the kitchen, and we talked. Jack told me that he had seen his mother and her boyfriend with some bags of stuff that he thought was sugar. He asked about it, and his mother's boyfriend hit him. He said that his mother gets upset if Jack asks too many questions or draws attention to them when they're out in public."

Chief White was taking notes. "I understand. I'll have this checked out. You should have come to the police sooner. You say that the mother is moving?"

I nodded. "Ms. Cramer said that she got a new position south of the border. I don't know when they're planning to move."

Chief White called in two officers and explained the situation to them. He told them to start digging into the matter and figure out how to handle everything. After that Dawn and I were taken to separate rooms and processed into the system.

I had to strip and be checked for weapons. Afterward I was photographed and fingerprinted. A male officer was leading me to a holding cell when a female officer stopped him. "We found some marijuana and mushrooms in the pocket of the female perp. Better test him."

I was taken to a bathroom and told to pee into a small jar. I knew what they would find when they tested it, so I confessed. "I smoked pot earlier. I took mushrooms in the last month. I've smoked pot a number of times over the last month."

The male officer nodded and led me to a holding cell. Dawn was put into one beside me. We were both charged with trespassing, conspiracy to incite riot, ingestion of controlled substances, disorderly conduct, and resisting arrest. Dawn was also charged with possession of a controlled substance.

Dawn's parents showed up first. Her father was over six feet tall and heavily muscled. His face was red, and his eyes were fierce. Dr. Cassandra Larkspur looked kind and gentle. She was all smiles and hugs for her poor daughter.

"Please, Officer Eselschmuck. She is from a well-to-do family. I know my sweet angel would never be mixed up with this sort of behavior if it wasn't for bad influences. I'm a psychologist. Can't we just let this matter go and I'll get to the bottom of things? I promise she'll get the help she needs."

"Ma'am, it's out of my hands. You'll receive word about trials or anything else that must occur. I would suggest talking to the judge when your daughter goes to trial."

I knew an act when I saw one – and Cassandra Larkspur didn't have me fooled. Dawn was in major trouble. Her father put a hand on her shoulder and guided her away. I watched her wince.

"I'm sorry, Dad. Things got out of control. I was just trying to help some people." Dawn choked back tears.

"Not half so sorry as you'll be when I get you home. Keep walking. The sooner we get out of here the better." Mr. Larkspur replied.

My parents appeared next. I was let out of my cell, and my mother ran over and hugged me. "Oh, my poor baby. I was so worried when I heard you got caught up in this mess. I'm certain that you and Dawn had nothing to do with any of this."

My father signed some papers and indicated that he was my legal representative. He asked the officers numerous questions and then my parents walked out of the station with me trailing behind them.

No one said a further word to me until we arrived home. I walked into the living room, and my father shoved me to the floor from behind. I stood up and he slapped me hard enough to knock me back down.

"Dammit, you pathetic, liberal, pinko piece of crap! How could you get involved in this? Do you care nothing about my reputation in this community or the reputation of your mother? What the Hell were you doing there in the park with that feral scum? And when the Hell did you start taking drugs?"

I began to cry. I couldn't help it. "That scum, as you call them, are my friends and Dawn's. We..."

"Shut up!" My father roared as my mother pulled me from the floor and shoved me down onto the couch. "Dammit, Francis! You're stuck in the mess that you created. Now, so are your mother and I. Crying like a baby isn't going to get you a lighter sentence. No one cares about how upset you are. You and Dawn were in a place you know you shouldn't have been, consorting with people with whom you have no business associating. My colleagues and I prosecute that kind of trash in the courts. You were raised to better standard, and I damned well expect you to live up to it!"

"I was just trying to..."

"You just shut up and listen, Francis Leslie Ahriman! I don't know what this Cyrus crap is about, but that isn't your name. We gave you a fine name. You'll use it and not some criminal alias."

I tried standing up and was again slapped. I stayed put on the couch rubbing my jaw. My father began pacing.

"There are reasons that the city makes ordinances like the one against concerts in the park. The violence you caused tonight happened all too often before that ordinance. I know people who had to defend that garbage you're calling friends. I prosecuted more cases than you can count because of societal refuse like that. If those supposed adult people would behave like humans instead of animals, then there would be no need to prohibit concerts. You and Dawn are better than they are. You were raised better, and in civilized homes. You are never to associate with that type of garbage again. Do you understand me? Now get up to your room and stay there. I'll have your meals brought to the door. You'll stay in your room except to use the bathroom until I can figure a way out of this mess and set up your arraignment hearing. Neither your mother nor I want to look at you. Now go."

I stood and began walking to my room. As I walked away my mother had her say. "I knew you'd find a way to screw up. You can't even hold a simple babysitting job without screwing everything up. They told us that you might have endangered the welfare of a small child because you didn't have the sense to call for help when you knew it was needed."

I turned in a fury. "You and he told me that if I had any problems, I was to handle them myself. So, I did. I'll be in my room. I hate you both. You can slap me until blood comes out of my ears and I will still hate you both."

I stormed upstairs and closed the door. After making sure they weren't coming in to hit me more, I collapsed on my bed and sobbed. I cried until I had to vomit, which I did in my trashcan. Then I sobbed some more.

I finally curled into a ball on the floor near my door. As I fell asleep, I overheard Mrs. Ferrigno laying into my parents.

"I quit. You hear me, I am done. I should have left a long time ago. The way you treat Francis is terrible. I will not work for child abusers, and you both are abusive to him. You tell him he's worthless. You tell him he has to be a lawyer or a scientist because you are. You never listen to him. He is a gentle and compassionate soul. He got into trouble because he cares too much about people you spit on. Well, you better figure it out because I am done. I will leave tomorrow."

I smiled a bit, although my mouth and face stung, and fell asleep as best I could. I woke up every so often, and finally I stood and walked to my closet. I found my baseball bat and put it beside me. I slept better after that.

CHAPTER TWENTY-FOUR

I woke up to a light knock at the door. Mrs. Ferrigno was bringing me breakfast.

"Cyrus," she placed a tray of melon with cottage cheese, pancakes, sausages, and coffee on my desk, "you stood up for your beliefs. That's important. That's the mark of you being a man instead of a boy in my eyes. I am leaving this morning."

"I know." I hugged her. "I heard you telling them last night."

"My leaving isn't your fault. I share some of your beliefs in the way the world should be. I am certain we have our differences, but as you age your views will change. It happens naturally. You are young yet. You'll find many more causes that will draw your attention. Never stop fighting."

We hugged again and she departed. I ate in silence and thought about Dawn. I missed her. I thought about everything Get Lost Jimmy had told us. I took out my sketch book and began drawing Swee'pea from memory.

My mother came up and took my tray a half hour later. "Francis, we lost our tempers last night. I'm sorry. He shouldn't have hit you. Things have been said that shouldn't have been said. We just want you to be independent, but also to know your place in society."

I turned my back to her and looked out the window. I said

nothing. She walked out and closed the door behind her.

The week passed with meals being brought by my mother and the dishes retrieved. I refused to speak to her. My father never came to my room. I began doing pushups and crunches every day and shadow boxing. I sketched and wrote poetry. I had no idea what was going to happen to me. People came and went downstairs.

At the end of the week, I was laying on my bed looking at the Christmas edition of *Snack Trays*. I tossed the magazine across the room toward my cherry wood desk, missing the desktop and landing it on my office chair. I eased myself off the bed and looked at the calendar on my wall. July 17th, 1993. I had been incarcerated in my room for a full seven days. My jaws were less sore, but my internal rage was increasing.

I ambled over to the window and opened my black and grey checkered curtains. Staring out the bay window at the lush green trees, and perfectly manicured lawn, I sighed a deep mooing sound reminiscent of a bull in heat. A bull in heat was an apt description of my mental and physical state.

I turned my ceiling fan to high, grabbed my black sketch book, and was sketching when a loud knock on the door interrupted me. I grabbed my baseball bat and opened it. Standing there was Chief White. I stepped aside and he entered.

I glared at him. "What? What do you want, Officer, sir!"

"We need to talk, Cyrus. Yes, I know your real name is Francis Leslie, but I can respect your desire to change that name. Regardless of what you may think, I'm not your enemy. I'm sorry, but we had no choice other than to put a stop to that concert. We couldn't just arrest the agitators without stopping everything else. You think that the police have it in for the people in the park because they're homeless, or because of their race, or whatever it is you think. You're as wrong as a body can be."

"How am I wrong? I saw what you did. I see what you do. I hear about it on the news and read about it in the papers. You don't understand and neither does any other adult. This isn't your world anymore. It belongs to us. We are the future so you can either lend a hand or get out of the way."

"Cyrus," Chief White sat on my chair, so I sat on my bed. He looked tired. "I don't hate the homeless and I don't hate the young people who live in that park. I expect everyone to behave. I'm paid to see that they do. They know the rules of the game and they know the consequences if they break those rules. I know that you don't understand this, and I can't make you understand it. So, enough small talk. Let's get down to business."

I shrugged. "Like I asked you. What do you want?"

"You're in trouble. So is Dawn Larkspur. You're both in serious trouble here. You might have to do time. Many of the teens in the park *will* be doing hard time. Some will be tried as adults for committing assault. Others will be in juvenile hall until they are eighteen. If I can help you both, I will. I'll do everything in my power to keep you out of the system and to have your records expunged when you turn eighteen."

"In exchange for what?"

"Before we get to that, I do have some good news for you."

I raised my eyebrows. "Oh? Like what?"

"We found the Cramer boy and he's safe. We arrested his mother, but we couldn't locate her boyfriend. There were no drugs in her house, but our K-9 unit detected trace amounts of heroin in the walk-in closet of her bedroom. We are interrogating her, and she will eventually give everything up. Your young friend will be safe. We have him stashed with a family for now, and we have a place where he will be able to grow and thrive. Which brings me to my proposition."

"Yeah?" I nodded. "Go on."

"There's a place out of state where you can do your time. Far out of state. Minnesota, in fact. It'd better than the JDC."

"Drop dead. I can handle juvie. I won't let you keep me away from Dawn. I won't let you force me into some place that wants to make me into a clone of my parents, either."

Chief White threw back his head and let go with a hearty laugh. "No wonder you and she get along so well. You're two of a kind, you are. She said almost exactly the same thing. Only her suggestion was anatomically impossible."

"Good. Then take your offer and shove it."

"I admire your scrap, Cyrus. I truly do admire your pluck. The problem here is that you don't have a choice. If you take my offer, you will only get a year probation. I can guarantee that. After you turn eighteen your record will be clean. The same holds for Dawn."

"Let's say I admire how you have me by the balls here. I need to ask you something. Why in the f...why are you doing this, Chief? Why do you care what happens to us?"

"It's a return favor. I like bratwurst. I like them with spicy onions and brown mustard in grinder rolls. Mrs. White tells me not to eat them because I have to watch my weight and my cholesterol. We all have our battles in life, Cyrus. We all have our causes and rebellions."

"I'll think about it."

"You have twenty-four hours to decide. So does Dawn. I already spoke to her."

"Is she OK?"

"Nothing that time and some salve won't take care of. I did speak to her parents about their reactions to her behavior. I'll speak to yours if you like."

"No. I can handle my father myself. My mother, too."

Chief White left and I sat at my desk and began sketching Jack from memory. He was going to be safe. The thought brought tears to my eyes. There was another knock, and the door opened. My father walked in, and I grabbed my baseball bat and stood facing him. He put his hands in the air to either side which I thought was a stupid move since I was armed.

"Hit me again and I will defend myself. If I'm going to juvie, what's one more charge on my record?" I felt a fury rising in me that had been building all week. "I'm not your damned punching bag. You can take your racist, conservative, narrow-minded, elitist crap and go to Hell!"

My father stepped forward and I readied my stance. "I'll leave then. You need to come downstairs...please. There is someone who needs to speak with you."

I allowed my father a decent lead and then followed with the bat in my hand. As I walked into the living room, I saw Dawn's mother and father sitting on the couch. I made a move toward Dawn's father, but it was checked. My father pointed toward the kitchen.

"In there, please. The Larkspurs were just leaving."

I walked into the kitchen, and my eyes widened. Sitting at the table drinking coffee was Top Cat. I took a minute to get my mind straight and sat on a chair across from him.

"Top Cat!? What are you doing here? How did you know where I lived?" My chest felt tight, and a throbbing started in my temples.

Top Cat raised a finger to his lips. "Keep it down, dude. Not everyone knows everything in this place." He handed me a business card. It read: *Dr. Shmuel Tetley: Music Therapy, Clinical Research, Child Advocate.*

I looked up from the card, "who is Shmuel Tetley?"

Top Cat winked at me, "that would be me."

"So, you're a fraud? What's going on here?"

"Fraud? Who's the dude that's been going around this summer calling himself Cyrus? You haven't been completely upfront with me or a lot of other people, you know."

"Who are you? I mean who are you really?"

"Right now, dude, I'm as close to an earthly savior as you are likely to get. I have some matters of importance to discuss with you."

I stood, poured myself a coffee, added cream and sugar, and sat. I couldn't formulate the words I needed. I took a sip of my coffee and tried again. "I take it you know what occurred."

"Sure. I tried to warn you and Dawn in advance."

"You know what? Go to Hell, OK? You act like there was any way of knowing what was going to happen. We tried to remind everyone to be peaceful and to play it cool. That rout of skinheads screwed everything up. They destroyed a great thing that we had going, man."

Top Cat gave me a solemn look. "As they always do and always will. I've been observing you this summer, Cyrus. The truth of the matter is that if it came to a fair one, you versus any one of those baldies, it *would be* a rout. You'd clean the floor with the biggest of them. The problem is that it would never be a fair one. You have yet to learn that fact."

"What do you want from me? First you sound like you don't think I should fight for what I believe, and then you say that in a fight I'd win."

176

Top Cat drank coffee and sighed. "You're correct. I do want something. But let's clear up a few facts here first. I believe in fighting for what you believe; provided, of course, that you are absolutely certain you're right. I believe that it is the solemn duty and obligation of the younger generations to bring about whatever change they can in society. You can't always win, though. You made a change for the better with the bratwurst coup. You failed with the concert. The latter was doomed from the start, but I admire your pluck in trying."

I shook my head, confused. "Are you for me and Dawn or against us? I can't keep up with you here."

"For you. Against you. Those aren't the only choices, you know? Or, maybe, you don't know. You're smart and so is Dawn. I forget that you're probably still thinking in a binary way. That only changes with age."

"So, what do you want?" I drank coffee.

"Well, if we can put the agro-fest on simmer for a bit, I need your help. I think a bit of background is in order first. I am involved with a facility in the upper-Midwest. I don't run everything, but I help to finance the place. It's called Happy House, and it serves youth who are abused, abandoned, or otherwise in trouble. We don't get many youths from the upper-socioeconomic sphere. Those we do serve are in the category of abused or abandoned. You and Dawn would be the first upper-middle class criminals with whom we worked. Of course, I believe that you and she also fit the other categories as well. Not exactly, but close enough."

I pondered what he had just told me. "So, this is what? An alternative to prison? A halfway house?"

"It is, and it isn't. There is a fifty-acre grounds with multiple cabins. The main building is Happy House itself. There are educational facilities, a gym with a running track, an indoor pool, hiking paths, and therapeutic sessions. The older youths actually run the place under the guidance of adults. The education and therapy aren't optional, and any off-campus activities are chaperoned. However, we do have a large kitchen and there are three meals a day plus a commissary if you earn points towards purchases."

"It sounds interesting." I felt the tension ease in my head and chest. "So, are you suggesting that I live at this place?"

"I am suggesting that you live at Happy House. That Dawn lives at Happy House. We need people with vision to help the facility grow; people who can transpose between the various social orders and help make the place a success on all levels."

"I'd consider it. According to Chief White, I have less than twenty-four hours to decide. The problem for me is this. I can't go there alone. I won't. Dawn taught me a lot of things about myself this summer. She's really smart. She knows more than she lets on. She knew one thing long before I ever knew it; that she's the best friend I ever had. I won't take your offer unless she does, and I need to hear her say it."

"I had a feeling you'd say that. I spoke to Dawn earlier this morning. She said I needed to tell you that Dr. Larkspur is against this whole idea. She believes that places like Happy House shouldn't exist. She believes that our approach is wrong, and that the criminal youths we serve need more discipline and incarceration. Dawn said that I had to emphasize that her parents are against this entire deal. By the way, your folks aren't what I would call jazzed by it, either. They agree that it is better than you going to JDC for a few years."

I laughed. "That's what I mean about Dawn. She knew that telling me this would guarantee an affirmative response from me. Fine, Top – er, Dr. Tetley. You win. If Dawn is in, I'm all in."

"Excellent. Now that we have that cleared up, I need your help more immediately. Yours and Dawns. There's a new client and he has had a hard time of it. Plus, he has a minor health issue that needs to be addressed."

"That's your arena, man. We're not doctors. How could we possibly help you?" I shook my head.

"Well, the boy just turned six yesterday. He had to be taken from his home due to severe abuse and certain criminal activity on the part of his mother and her boyfriend. The problem is that he doesn't trust anyone except me. The other problem is that when he is offered food, he only wants to eat pizza, cheeseburgers, snack cakes, and the like. He's bordering on corpulence, and if he doesn't learn to eat healthier, he is going to have future issues."

"How is that mine and Dawn's problem? How do we help with that?"

"Seeing as you both caused his eating issues; I should think you might explain to him about a balanced diet."

I scowled, "We caused...you son of a bitch." I laughed hard. "Why didn't you just tell me that Jack was safe? Where is he? Can we see him?"

"That's what I'm trying to explain, dude. Yes, you both can see him. You're going to have to see him. He's in a foster home at the moment, but in a week, I am taking a train back to Minnesota. You, Dawn, and Jack will be on that train."

"So, you want us to transport him for you? With you chaperoning us?"

Top Cat shook his head, "I thought you were brighter than this. I guess I have to spell things out. At the facilities we have the main house wherein live the youngest residents. That's also where the kitchen is located and many of the classrooms. There are unisex cabins on the property, and a few co-ed cabins for those we feel can handle that arrangement. You and Dawn will be assigned to a co-ed cabin, but not to the same sleeping quarters. I am sure that you and she have already explored that part of your relationship, and I know that you both take drugs. That's over for now. You can have a relationship and build something healthy for yourselves. We have counselors who can hold individual as well as couple's sessions. You'll attend those. What we need is people who Jack Flash trusts in order to help him settle in. Other than me, the only two people he is likely to trust completely are you and Dawn."

"So, we're going to be his guardians? We're going to get to take care of him again?"

"By George, I think he's got it."

I laughed. "That sounds great. What happens after...I mean... when he..."

Top Cat interrupted me, "He won't. His mother is going away for long enough that he will be my age before she's released. The cops haven't found the boyfriend yet, but they will."

"Can Dawn and I stay with Jack until he's done with high school?"

"One day at a time, dude. I think that might be possible, but let's take this slow. You and she still have a lot of problems to work out yourselves."

"What problems? It sounds like my major problems were just solved. I'm free of my parents and their pretentious crap. I'm going to a place where I can be with Dawn every day and can take care of Jack. You say that there are educational facilities which I imagine means that I can continue with my art and writing. That's all I really need."

"Oh, there are serious issues involved here, dude. You're still on probation and so is Dawn. Believe me, this isn't going to be all fun and games. I'm trying to avoid the heavy stuff for now, but it is clear that you have a great deal of anger boiling over inside of you. So does Dawn. I don't want to place judgements, and from what I've heard this past week I think that the anger is to some degree righteous. It still has to be addressed and dealt with at a therapeutic level."

"Why? If you get me and Dawn away from this environment where people act like they're better than others, if you give us a fair shot at having some sense of self-determination, I don't see how the anger inside of us won't lessen a great deal. Yes, I hate my parents. I also love them at the same time. It's confusing. I think if I could move somewhere else and live my life on my own terms, things would be vastly improved. You're offering me that opportunity."

Top Cat shook his head and gave me a serious look. "You don't understand this yet, Cyrus, but if you want others to see you the way you want to be seen, then you must see yourself that way. You have to build character in yourself, discipline in yourself, determination in yourself. You have got to learn to survive with dignity, no matter how tough the world around you may be. You think you already know how to do that, but there's so much more to learn. It will come naturally with age, and it will come with therapy and education."

"I'm in. Let's do it." I shook hands with Top Cat.

CHAPTER TWENTY-FIVE

I picked up my baseball bat and headed to the living room. Top Cat followed me shaking his head and sighing. The Larkspurs were gone, and my parents were seated on the couch.

Top Cat looked at the three of us. "I think we've come to terms. I'll be in touch in the next couple of days." He started to leave, and then turned around. "There is one thing I need to say...I want to say...before I go. Your son is standing here with a weapon in his hands. He doesn't fully understand how out of control he actually is. He thinks he's getting everything that he wants in life. He may be, but he is a hair-trigger from something far worse than any of you can possibly imagine. The reason for that...anyway a major reason for that...rest squarely on the two of you. You have both done more damage to your reputation than your son could ever cause. You have convinced him that he's worth nothing unless he meets some arbitrary standard of respectability that you both set. You are both just as damaged as he is. I don't know what the root of your problems are, and at the moment I find it hard to give a damn. I will not watch your son be hurt that way any longer. Whatever else he is, he's my friend. I plan to let the Larkspurs know the same about Dawn. Good day to you." Top Cat walked out the door and closed it behind him.

My mother and father looked at me standing there with the bat in my hands, ready in case they tried anything foolish. My parents had a look of fear in their eyes, and I must admit that it was one of the best looks I had ever seen from them.

My mother looked up at me. "So, I take it you agreed to attend this place. It sounds like you have a kindred spirit in that man. I don't buy what he just said, but, in some ways, I am glad that you agreed to this plan. You'll be safer there until all of this blows over and our family's reputation is restored in this community. I still think that some time in a juvenile facility would be better for you. You'd get discipline and maybe you'd come to realize your place in society. However juvenile hall would be a more permanent stain on our family. Maybe after a year at this Happy House place you can return home and your father can set you up with a part-time position in his firm."

I scowled. "Incredible! You still don't get it, do you? I'm not coming back in a year, or five years, or ten. He's right. You've spent years telling me what a screw-up I am. Now you have what you preordained. I'm a screw-up. You lost me a long time ago, and I'm not going to suddenly change who I am. I'm never going to become a clone of you two. Deal with it!"

My father started to stand and thought better of it. He raised his hands in surrender as I moved the bat in my hands. "Son, I apologize. I've never looked at you as a man before. I can see now that you are becoming a man instead of being the boy I always saw. You're a decent man who has to go his own way. You definitely have some of my fire in you. I wish I understood why you feel as you do about so many matters but suffice it to say that I understand this much. You'll never be a corporate raider, or a prosecuting attorney. You'll never accept the conservative standpoint, and you'll always care too much about people who are beneath you socially. That's who you are, and I can accept you that way. I love you. You're my son."

"I love you too. Both of you. I don't love your lifestyle, although I admit that it has some perks. I definitely don't love your position of superiority over those who were dealt an unlucky hand in life. Am I allowed to come and go now? Am I still confined to the house?"

My mother sat crying, shaking, and losing her composure. My father sighed. "You're welcome to come and go as you please. Do not get into further trouble. Please."

I turned and walked upstairs. Dressing in jeans and a muscle shirt, I put on my socks, combat boots, and wrapped a bandana around my head. I grabbed my pack and headed downstairs. By the time I returned to the living room, my parents were gone. I hadn't heard them leave, but I wasn't listening that hard. I put on my portable CD player and cranked up a CD of "Eye for an Eye" by Corrosion of Conformity.

I was halfway to Dawn's when I saw her walking my way dressed in loose fitting shorts, a t-shirt, and high-top converse sneakers. She was listening to a CD as well. I hit stop on my player and hung my earphones around my neck. She did the same.

I approached, silently hugged her, and patted her on the butt. She winced and pulled away. I saw fear in her eyes, as she began to cry. I moved closer to her, and she backed away.

"What's the matter? I'm not going to hurt you. I was going to hold you. I've missed being with you." I looked for a place to sit. There was a bench near the corner, and I sat patting the seat beside me.

Dawn shook her head and remained standing. "What the hell

do you think is the matter!? Dammit, keep your hands off my ass. Keep your hands off of *me*."

I sighed. "I knew it was too good to last. I thought, from what Top Cat said, that you wanted to attend this place with me. That you wanted me to be with you. I thought that you wanted to be a couple."

"Cyrus, I'm fifteen years old. I don't know *what* the hell I want right now. Neither do you. I think we don't have a choice about taking Top Cat's offer. It sounds good, and it beats the alternative. As for being with you, I want that. OK? But you have to respect my space. I think we have a good chance together. I just..." She took a breath and tried to compose herself. Her voice softened. "I'm sorry. My dad really lit me up this week. Like, every day. He screamed and raged and tore my ass up until two days ago. He's lucky Chief White didn't run him in. It was a near thing, but I said I won't press charges. I guess that doesn't matter, actually. The cops can press charges without me. But, my saying I wouldn't, it kept my dad out of jail."

I took a deep breath and let it out slowly. "Why would you protect him like that? You want that I should deal with him instead? I promised Top Cat, Chief White, and my parents that I'd stay out of trouble, but screw it. Give me the word and I'll go kick your father's ass into the next century."

Dawn shook her head. "You will do no such thing, Francis Leslie Ahriman! Why the hell do you think I protected him? That bruise on your face is fading, but it's there. Why don't you have *your* parents arrested? You love them, right? I love my parents, too. I hate them, but I love them. If that makes any sense. Anyway, I handled everything with Mom and Dad."

I stood. "Handled it how?"

"I told them both where to go. Chief White was standing

there, so they had to take it. I made it clear that I'm an adult now. If they so much as lift a finger toward me, I'll call the cops and ask for Chief White."

"Good for you. I told my parents off, as well. In spades. My mother doesn't get it, but I think my father is starting to."

Dawn and I put our CD players in our packs and began walking. I tried to change the mood a bit. "I was listening to Corrosion of Conformity. You?"

"The Exploited. I had it up as loud as I could tolerate."

"That's the best way to let it all out." I smiled at her, and she smiled back.

We were walking aimlessly. She took my hand but that was all. I didn't know what more to say other than I loved her, and she knew that already. I looked up at one point and realized that we were in Jack's neighborhood. Four police officers were carrying items out of the house. They had boxes of clothes, some toys, and a number of books. A large, drunken, unshaved man came storming toward them.

"What the hell do you think you're doing? That stuff belongs to my girlfriend and her son. You can't take it without a warrant."

A female police officer stepped forward and put a hand on the man's chest. "We have a court order. If you need to see it, I'll show it to you, but please settle down."

The man shoved past her and walked directly toward me and Dawn. "What are you looking at, boy? Get off my sidewalk."

"It isn't your sidewalk, creep." I lowered my center of gravity and set my feet. Dawn backed away.

"I said get the hell off my street. Who are you?" The man slurred.

"I'm your worst nightmare, you rancid son of a bitch. My

name is Cyrus, and I babysat for that boy you beat up. You want to try hitting me!?"

The man squared off with me, and I was about to start swinging. Dawn moved quickly and grabbed me from behind. Two cops moved forward to stop us, but before they got there the guy took a swing at me. He hit me in the solar plexus. Dawn let go of me, and I backed off gasping for air.

The man tried swinging at Dawn, but she backed away. She moved forward and drove a hard one into the man's gut followed by a knee to his crotch. He doubled over gasping. Two cops were standing behind him with their hands on their guns. As Dawn retreated toward me, the man reached behind and under his shirt. He produced a gun, and I grabbed Dawn and tossed her into a nearby yard, landing on top of her.

Before he could fire, one of the cops shot him in the shoulder. He turned and she shot him in the head. I grabbed Dawn and pulled her close. The entire action from him punching me to the police officer killing him took about one tenth of the time it took to write about it. It was nothing like the movies, or detective novels make it out to be. I rolled off of Dawn and we huddled together terrified.

One of the other officers approached us. "It would be a good idea if you two weren't here. There are already people coming out of the houses. In fact, son, it would be better that you two were never here. You understand?"

"I do."

Dawn and I took off running past houses where people had exited in response to the chaos and the shooting. Police were shouting orders, and several more police cars and an ambulance arrived as we turned a corner. I was in a daze, and Dawn was blanching. We were five blocks away when she stopped and vomited in the gutter. I tried holding her, but she shoved me away. I took several deep breaths and tried to steady myself. I couldn't. I was certain that I would have a bruise where I had been punched. I couldn't clear the image from my head of seeing someone shot and killed. It really wasn't like in the movies. It was cleaner and more efficient in a way, but it was also terrifying. Seeing an actor on a screen allowed my mind to pretend that what I was seeing wasn't real. I couldn't pretend with this, and I couldn't get past the thought that if I hadn't been trying to fight it might not have happened at all.

Dawn and I started walking toward the park. She stopped and turned me toward her. "Do you need anything, Cyrus? A doctor? That was one hell of a punch you took."

"I'm alright. You know how to handle yourself when it comes to it. Thank you."

"Nobody, and I mean nobody, punches my boyfriend, and gets to walk away from it without repercussions. Anyway, you'd have gotten us both arrested again. You have a temper on you."

"What, and you don't?"

"Top Cat says we both do. I don't know about him, but he's all we have at the moment."

"I think he's solid. He needs us as much as we need him right now. I agree that he confuses me, but I think deep down he understands us."

Dawn grabbed me and held on tight around my waist, her face buried in my chest. "I can't believe what just happened." Dawn started sobbing. "That guy would have killed us. The cops had to shoot him, I know that, but I've never seen anything like that except on TV or in a movie."

"I don't want to talk about it. I want to forget it as soon as possible." I held her and stroked her hair.

As Dawn and I entered the park, Hetty ambled by pushing a cart. "Hey. Aren't you two the ones who put on that concert?"

Dawn nodded. I forced a smile. "That was us, Hetty. Sorry it turned out so bad."

Hetty nodded at me. "You tried. Most of us older folk just got questioned and let go. Bunch of kids got arrested, but not all. It happens. Can't win them all. You got a few bucks? I need lunch."

"Stay here with Dawn, I'll get you a couple of bratwursts and a Coke."

"With mustard, and sauerkraut. Thank you." Hetty stood chatting with Dawn until I returned.

Dawn and I walked to a corner deli. She went to the bathroom and cleaned up. When she emerged wearing a clean t-shirt, we ordered soup and sandwiches. As we were eating a voice came over the radio through the speaker system. "That was Mahler's Symphony Number 5. You're listening to WTLK radio. This is The Schmaltz coming at you with a special request. A caller all the way from Minnesota asked me to play Kindertotenlieder for a couple he met this summer."

I looked at Dawn and smiled. "I guess Uncle Don is back in business."

"Sounds like it. Care to dance?"

"If you like. I don't want to touch you if you don't want."

"Give me time, Cyrus. I'll need space and time to deal with everything that's happened. My mom knows some things anyway, and that's one of them. Trauma recovery takes space and time. I'll let you know when it's OK and when it's not OK to hold me. Now, do you want to dance or not?"

We stood and slow danced by our table. It was a long piece of music, and after a while we sat and finished our food. I paid the bill and we exited. The weather was dark, grey, and overcast which matched how I was feeling inside.

"Would you come home with me? Dawn asked. "I don't want any trouble if my parents are home, but I'd feel better if you were there with me."

"Sure. I'll help you pack, and then you can come over and help me." I put out my arms, and Dawn hugged me.

Once we arrived at her house, we found a note on the side table in the foyer. Her parents were out until late. We headed upstairs, took three suitcases from her closet, and neatly packed every item of clothing she owned except for a few outfits she wanted for the next few days. I took her DVD collection and stashed them under some sweatshirts.

Dawn sighed. "I want to keep those, but after everything this past week, part of me doesn't. I think I will for now."

"We could watch one if you want to."

Dawn shook her head. "Not right now. I'm not in the mood. I need time to separate that stuff from what happened with my parents."

I held her hands. "I understand. I'm sorry. It was insensitive of me to ask."

"Cyrus, we're both going to need tie to figure out a lot of things. It won't happen overnight. I think we both have triggers and issues that get set off. If we aren't careful, we'll hurt each other. But I don't want to walk on eggshells around you, either. Or vice versa."

"I get it. I agree."

"We'll watch those one day. I promise. It won't always be this way. Life will get better. I just need space right now. Space to really process everything that happened."

"I understand. I was actually thinking that we should take a break from sex for a while. I think we need to take a break from a lot of stuff. We need to focus on Jack."

"And ourselves. And each other." Dawn smiled at me. "I agree. We need to figure out if we actually like being with each other outside of sex and the constant activity from the last couple of months. When life is dull and full of homework and chores, do we still want to be around each other? I mean, it was a great summer, and I love you so much. I just..."

"I know. I think so, too, I think we have a lot in common, and I think we'll make it. Top Cat might be right though, there's a lot we need to figure out together and separately."

Dawn and I hugged, and she finished with her packing. We walked to my house, and I packed my clothes, art supplies and all my books. My parents still weren't home. I took most of my magazines and asked Dawn to leave them where the remaining kids in the woods might find them. I no longer felt the need to look at pictures when I had the real deal standing beside me.

CHAPTER TWENTY-SIX

Dawn and I stopped in my kitchen and had some cookies and milk. I wasn't anxious to be home, but I didn't want to stress out Dawn, either.

"I was thinking, maybe we could head to the park and then the mall. I have all the money from babysitting, and I don't know that I'll be able to spend it where we're heading. I won't need the same kind of stuff I needed at VHI in any case. I was thinking that we should load up on toiletries, and perfume and aftershave, and like that. Maybe we could buy some magazines or something for the train ride."

Dawn nodded. "That sounds like a good idea. I'd even let you buy me dinner."

The phone rang. "Hello? Ahriman residence."

"This is Dr. Tetley, sir."

"What's up, TC?" I smiled at Dawn.

"Oh, it's you. You sound like your father. Yeah, dude, I need you to go pick up Dawn and both of you be at the park in an hour. We have business with a munchkin."

"She's with me now, and we'll be there in thirty minutes." I hung up.

"He wants us to meet up with him at the park. He has Jack with him."

Dawn smiled as big as I'd seen all day. She stepped in and hugged me until my ribs almost gave out. "Let's go."

Dawn and I stopped on the way to get Cokes. As much as I was trying, my mind wouldn't stop replaying the shooting. I stopped outside the corner store and leaned against the wall, shaking, and trying not to cry.

Dawn tried to hug me, but I shrugged her off. "I'm fine. I just..."

"Words aren't necessary, Cyrus. It's not going to be easy. I can't tell you to be strong because I'm not strong right now."

Ten minutes later we entered the park and were walking toward the garden path when a voice behind us boomed. "Stop right there, kids."

We turned and Chief White was glaring at us. "There was a shooting earlier. The reports from my officers indicate that the man was inebriated and resisting. He drew a gun and one of them was forced to kill him. However, reports from people in the neighborhood indicate that two individuals matching your basic descriptions were seen running from the area. Tell me you two were not there."

Dawn turned ashen. I took a deep breath and let it out. "I'm sorry, sir, we didn't mean to..."

Chief White interrupted me. "When an officer of the law gives you an order, son, you best obey it."

"What are you..."

"Mr. Ahriman. Ms. Larkspur. I. Said. Tell. Me. You. Were. Not. There."

I began to sob, and then it struck me what Chief White wanted. "We were not there, Chief White, sir."

Dawn caught on fast. "We were not there, sir."

"Good. I'll close that lead then. Off the record, welcome to the big leagues. It doesn't get any easier, and it is going to get harder. I'm glad those two weren't you, but if they had been I'd guess it was just bad timing and that you weren't in that area looking for trouble. I need to go get my lunch and return to the station."

Dawn collapsed onto a bench as Chief White turned and headed to the vendor's cart. I sat beside her and stared into space. The minute I thought everything was under control, it all went to hell once more. My stomach felt as if I needed to vomit, my heart was racing, I was sweating, and my temples throbbed."

We were sitting there when a loud, excited screech broke us from our reverie. "Cyrus! Dawn!" Jack Flash came flying toward us with his arms outstretched.

I stood and caught him in a midair hug. "Hey, Jack! I'm so glad to see you again." I set him down.

Dawn knelt and hugged Jack like a mother bear finding her lost cub. "You OK, buddy?"

Jack shrugged. "I'm OK. There's a lot of bad guys now and sometimes I don't sleep good because I have to fight them. I had to move away and I'm moving very far away soon. My new friend, Dean, took me shopping for winter clothes. He said that where I'm going the winter gets very cold. He said there might be snow up to my armpits."

Dawn nodded. "Cyrus and I are going there, too. We might need to buy our own winter clothes."

"I'm glad you decided that, dudes." Top Cat ambled over. "Cyrus, are you OK? You look sick."

"Can Dawn watch Jack? I need to talk to you, sir. It might take a while."

"Certainly. As long as they stay in my line of vision it will be fine."

Jack and Dawn sat on a bench, and he leaned against her. She snuggled him and listened to him chatter on. Top Cat and I retreated to a bench fifty feet away. I sat staring into space trying to figure out how to explain everything without getting me or Dawn into further trouble.

Top Cat looked over at me. "What's up?"

"Dawn and I were walking earlier. Just wandering aimlessly and talking about life and our relationship. We wound up in Jack's neighborhood. I promise that we weren't deliberately heading that way, but we wound up there. The police were taking boxes out of the Cramer household, and Jack's mother's boyfriend approached. He was drunk."

Top Cat look concerned. "I heard on the radio that there was a shooting in that area earlier."

"We saw it. The creep punched me. I...I admit that I antagonized him when I found out who he was. He hit me really hard. I'm fine. Dawn stepped up and kneed him in the safe deposit box, and he drew a gun. Before he could shoot, one of the officers opened fire and killed him."

"Jesus! I'm glad you're both OK."

"The officers told us to leave the area and not say anything to anyone. Chief White just saw us, and he is making a report that we weren't the kids seen running from the area."

Top Cat looked at me with compassion and then his eyes narrowed. "Boy, when I tell you and her to stay out of trouble, I mean it. I don't mean go and make everything worse. I don't mean get yourselves killed. I mean lay low and don't get into any trouble. You hearing me, boy?"

I started to sob again. "Yes, sir. I'm sorry. Please don't take back your offer. At least let Dawn go."

Top Cat reached over and pulled me toward him. He side-hugged me and let me cry. "I'm not taking back my offer. I know that you and Dawn weren't planning on that happening. No one ever does. It isn't like in the movies or books, huh? It's real and it's scary."

"I dried my face with my sleeve and let Top Cat hug me. "Yes, sir. It's something I can't unsee. I know I said I wouldn't tell anyone, but I had to tell you."

"I'm glad you did, dude. I'm glad you did. Can you do something for me from now on?"

"I promise, we'll stick to our houses, the mall and the park."

"I'd appreciate it, but that isn't what I wanted. Could you try being honest and up front with me from now on? Could you be that way with your teachers and counselors? You've spent the summer under an assumed name, and causing problems that are much bigger than you can handle. You encouraged a five-year-old to keep secrets from others. That's something else we need to discuss one day."

"I can't speak for Dawn, but I promise to try."

"So, what do we tell Jack? How do we let him know that this bastard is dead?"

I smiled a bit. "He's Jack Flash. Tell him that the superheroes beat the bad guys. That the bad guys won't be coming back again."

Top Cat laughed, "did I just hear you call the cops super-heroes? Yeah, boy, you'll make it. It's going to take a lot of work, but you'll make it."

We walked back to Dawn and Jack. Top Cat sat beside Jack as Dawn stood. "You OK, Cyrus?" Dawn asked.

"I guess. I told TC everything."

Dawn nodded. Good. Now it's your turn to spend time with

CHAPTER TWENTY-SIX

Jack. I need to talk to you myself, Top Cat.

Dawn and Top Cat walked toward the benches and Jack moved closer to me. "Cyrus, you promised that you'd never leave me. So did Dawn. You left me." Jack pouted and crossed his arms.

I had no choice, Jack. Neither did she. We aren't grownups, you know? We still have rules to follow. I will promise that other than having to be home, Dawn and I will be by your side as much as we can. If not us, someone else. You'll be safe."

Jack stood on the bench. "Give me a hug please."

I hugged Jack and sat him in my lap. "You and I need to talk about something, though. I'm not mad, and no one else is, but you can't live on a diet of snack cakes, hotdogs, French fries, and soda pop. You have to eat salads, veggies, fresh fruit, and a good balance of starch and protein. Otherwise, you'll bulk up. If you're exercising a lot, it's OK to eat more. However, you still want to watch the junk food."

"Top Cat already told me that. I don't like the kind of food Mommy made me eat."

"Jack, there's a difference between going overboard on health food and eating healthy. I suspect your mother had other reasons for insisting that you eat the way she made you eat. It doesn't matter. I think maybe we should ask Top Cat if we can take cooking classes together when we get to Happy House."

Jack curled up and yawned in my lap. Top Cat and Dawn returned. Her eyes were red, and she looked drawn. "He just fell asleep here. You OK?"

Dawn shrugged. "I will be. I'm sorry in advance but you and I already have homework due the first week of school."

I chuckled, "do we now? What homework?"

Top Cat gave me a serious look. "You and I will discuss it more on the train. I'm your friend, Mr. Ahriman, but I am also in charge here. It's time we got to work undoing the damage that has been done by and to you both."

CHAPTER TWENTY-SEVEN

I'm on a train heading west. We have a sleeper suite, and Dawn has her own bunk as do I. We've been riding for three days, and we arrive tomorrow. The shower is adequate, and the food is edible, but I miss what I left behind. Jack has been ecstatic and subdued by turns. He hangs on me and Dawn as much as possible, wanting to sit in our laps or maintain some point of contact. We can't leave him for a minute without him crying for us.

Jack spent the entire first two days in his seat watching the nation pass by outside the window. He naps in one bunk or the other and Dawn or I have to sit beside him in case he wakes up. He's going to need a lot of help, and I don't know if Dawn and I can provide it all. We're both struggling to keep it together ourselves.

The second day of our trip west, Top Cat called me into his compartment. I took a seat, and he poured us each some coffee from an urn. I sat in silence waiting for him to talk.

"Dawn tells me that you write poetry. She says that you're a gifted artist." Top Cat sipped his coffee, decided that it was the proper temperature, and took a bigger swig.

"I suppose. I'm no Ginsburg, or William Carlos Williams, but I suppose my poetry is OK. I'm no Modigliani or Chagall, either."

"No. You're Cyrus Ahriman. Which brings me to my first point. If you decide to write for a living, and I promise that being a professional isn't a money-making proposition, the name Cyrus Ahriman has an authorial ring to it. Then again so does, F.L. Ahriman or Frankie Ahriman."

"I guess. I despise Francis Leslie. I'm not effeminate."

Top Cat chuckled and then gave me a stern look. "I'll have you know that one of the coolest cats ever, Frank Sinatra, was named Francis. You can look it up. Furthermore, Leslie Nielson is a mighty funny guy, and didn't see a reason to change the name professionally. There are plenty of mobsters who'd drop you in a heartbeat and they don't mind the name Frankie. You can look that up as well."

I winced when he mentioned someone dropping me. "Dawn and I almost got dropped not so long ago. Can we not talk about that?"

"We don't have to right now. You are going to have to at some point with someone or more than one someone. You will have to deal with your emotions before they deal with you."

"Yeah. I guess." I stared out the window.

"My second point is this. I mentioned looking things up. You'll be doing a lot of that for three weeks after we arrive. I understand that you and Dawn didn't deliberately walk into that neighborhood and weren't looking for trouble. However, when trouble found you, your reaction was dangerous. It fits a pattern with you. I had to get your school records and Dawn's to transfer them. I took a peek. You've had a number of fights over the last few years. You never got in trouble for them because they were determined to not be your fault, but you have anger issues."

"OK. Your point being?"

"You and Dawn are in trouble. Not the trouble you've met over the years at the hands of your parents, but trouble nevertheless."

I sighed. "Explain that. What? Are we going to solitary confinement when we get there? Do you plan to make us clean the latrines?"

Top Cat laughed. "You've got a sharp tongue on you, boy. This isn't prison or the military. There's a library on the grounds. You and Dawn are both academically gifted in different ways. She's better at math than you. You have a greater artistic aptitude and get better grades on your essays. So, you and she will be spending three weeks writing a fifteen-page paper together on the second amendment. I want pros and cons. I want proper citations. I expect you to use correct punctuation and spelling. It has to be a proper academic report. You'll submit it to Mr. Robinson, the head of out English department."

"I can do that. I'm sure Dawn can do that. Why that subject if I'm allowed to ask? I don't have much interest in the law."

"No. You did however experience gun violence. So did Dawn. I think it would be good for both of you to explore the arguments pro and con about the ownership and use of weapons. It will help you in ways you have yet to understand."

"Fine. Is that everything?"

"Not quite. Cyrus, I want you to start journaling. I mean every day. I want you to write down your feelings, your poetry, your dreams, whatever you like. No one else has to see what you write, and that won't be graded. It will help you to become a better writer, and it will help you to find a path through the murky, mental confusion that you're experiencing."

"I'm not being smart, TC, but how do you understand so

much about me? How can you possibly know what confusion I'm feeling?" I felt some tears welling up.

"Cyrus, I wasn't always an adult. I have my own past. I saw my own fights and struggles. I understand because, whether you believe it or not, I've been there. That's one reason why I try to help others not have to go through it all. I'm on your side whether you accept that or not."

I stood to leave and then sat again. "There's something else I need to talk with you about."

"Yes?"

Dawn and I are doing our best by Jack. We will continue to do our best. However, she and I have talked, and we agree that Jack has needs we can't meet. Not yet. Maybe not ever. I'm trying to protect him, and I understand he was traumatized, but so was I. So was Dawn. It's like the blind leading the blind."

Top Cat poured more coffee for himself. "I'm pleased that you both see that. Jack is going to need a great deal of help over a great many years. Hate to be the bearer of bad news, but so are you and Dawn. If you can be Jack's friend and help care for him that will be enough. Which does bring up a point I still need to address."

I nodded. "Go ahead."

"Being his friend doesn't mean feeding him whatever he wants to eat. It definitely doesn't mean taking him to all night movies that are full of violence and adult situations. He's six. He needs to be treated accordingly."

"Jack told me that he wanted to be treated like a big kid. I thought about it and realized that when I was his age, I wanted that too."

"I am certain he does. I'm certain you did. Who doesn't at that age? There is something to be said for living in an age-appropriate environment. It isn't as easy as giving him what he thinks he wants. He doesn't actually know what he wants any more than you know what you want. You're still a creature of impulse. That will change with time."

I stood again and we shook hands. "Thank you. I can't promise that I'm going to do well all the time. I can't say that I like authority, or that I agree with everything that you just told me. You talked to me man to man, and I can respect that." I left and returned to Dawn's and my compartment. Dawn was asleep in her bunk with Jack curled up beside her.

I decided to finish this report before I start journaling. I'll write another one if anything occurs worth reporting. I'm not certain what the future holds for me, Dawn, or Jack. I'm sitting here thinking about Uncle Don and Get Lost Jimmy and his son Swee'pea, and all the homeless in the park. I learned a great deal from each of them. If this summer has taught me anything it is this. Our world is a foul and rancid place. More so than I ever imagined. I lack hope for the nation and for humanity in general. I struck a blow for freedom this summer, lost a bigger fight, and saw the devastation that fighting can bring about.

There will have to be significant changes made in our nation if anything is to improve. I may not live long enough to see those changes, but I plan to be on the front lines fighting. I hope Dawn will be standing beside me. Whether she is or not, when they take me out, I plan to go down swinging.

About the Author

With an early post-natal existence that made The Warriors look like The T-Birds in Grease, Ben Rose was born in western Oregon, and did time in Delaware and South Central Pennsylvania, before traveling for a couple of decades by bus, car, freight train, Amtrak, and foot in an effort to see America and find stories to write. He also sought himself but upon finding himself found that he didn't get along with himself if you dig the flip. He speaks fluent hipster as well as English. Ben is an ally of the LGBTQ+ Community, a supporter of human rights, and a believer in racial and gender equality. As one with High Functioning Autism, GAD, and PTSD, Ben has seen his share of hard traveling, abuse, and bullying which is reflected in his literary works. He currently resides in Pinellas County, FL with his beautiful better half and their cat.

You can connect with me on:

🐦 https://twitter.com/SobrietyStories

📘 https://m.facebook.com/profile.php/?id=100063950238834

🔗 https://www.instagram.com/benroseauthor

Also by Ben Rose

Life is hard when you're young. It's even harder when you are alienated and disenfranchised (homeless, abused, have psychological disorders, etc.) Drinking and drugs seem a great escape in the moment. Rebellion for the sake of rebellion seems good in the moment. The longer event horizon proves out that easy solutions are often toxic. It takes hard work and perseverance to reach a better place in life. My books describe this arc without actually concluding it because in life there is no happily ever after magic. It's an ongoing process.

Everybody But Us

Who gets a safe home to live in? Everybody But Us. Who gets parents to love and support them? Everybody But Us. Who gets all the breaks in life? Everybody But Us. What does FEBU stand for?

The Long Game

Vinnie II-Cazzo lives a life based on the hustle and the short con. When, at the age of 12, he meets Steph Baker, it's love at first sight for both of them. The romance is short lived as Steph, her mother, and her baby sister must flee domestic violence. Vinnie can't escape his need to find Steph again, and he begins playing a "long game" in an effort to locate her. In a world of hustle and jive, Vinnie soon discovers that the biggest mark he ever conned was himself.

Made in the USA
Middletown, DE
31 May 2024